BAD WITCH

A CAT MCKENZIE NOVEL

USA TODAY BESTSELLING AUTHOR

LAUREN DAWES

BAD WITCH

A CAT MCKENZIE NOVEL

And for Phil and Evie
...always.

1

ell me if you've heard this one before…

You come home from therapy, and there's a vampire at the door.

No?

I guess it only happens to me.

I slowed my steps as I approached my apartment, questions swirling around my head. Alistair de Champ turned when I was about ten feet away, his green eyes glowing in the artificial light of the hallway. At first glance, he looked like any other human would. On closer inspection, though, there was a layer of danger that surrounded him, and right now, my primitive brain was screaming at me to run.

Run like fucking Forrest.

I didn't want a vampire at my front door, and I certainly didn't want one inside my apartment. Moving closer, he seemed to stop breathing… well, maybe not *breathing*. He was a vampire, after all, but he did become very, very still.

Coming to a stop a healthy distance away, I swallowed. "I didn't take you for a Girl Scout." I made a show of glancing around at his feet. "No Thin Mints?"

He flashed me a fang-filled smile that I guessed he thought was comforting, but it only made me want to hide under my bed. As I waited for him to tell me what he was doing there, I let my eyes drift down his body, taking in the expensive charcoal gray suit, the crisp white dress shirt and his blood-red tie.

Hello, vampire movie cliché!

Tossing the keys in my hand for a moment, I began walking again. I hadn't seen him in a little over two weeks, not since my partner, Sawyer, and I went to visit his mistress on the hunt for information about a ticked-off vampire who had it in for me.

Yup, just another day in the life of Cat McKenzie.

"Mind telling me what you're doing here?" I asked cautiously.

His eyes drifted to the brace on my knee outside my jeans. Dammit, I hated to show weakness, especially to a supe.

"I have a message to deliver."

"Ever heard of a phone?"

He smiled without warmth. "It's not that kind of message."

"Okay, well, I'm here. What's the message?"

Alistair stared at me with all the emotion of a hungry shark. "Perhaps I should come in. I doubt you'd want your neighbors to overhear the conversation." When he saw me hesitate, he added, "I swear no harm will come to you by my hand if that is what's concerning you."

"A lot of things concern me," I replied curtly. "Teenage pregnancy. Gen Z's obsession with vanity, selfies, and IG filters. Running out of toilet paper during a zombie apocalypse. Just don't expect me to offer you a drink." When I slid the key into the lock, the teeth chattered along the tumbler, echoing like gunshots in my ears…

Or my death knells.

Christ, I hoped I was doing the right thing.

I stepped inside, placing my keys onto the hook on the wall, but Alistair stayed exactly where he was. Staring at me.

"Are you just going to stand there all night?"

"I can't come in until you invite me."

I bit my tongue to stop myself from laughing. "Seriously? That's a legitimate rule?"

"Unfortunately."

Peering over at the couch, I saw my back-up plan—Reaver—propped up against the arm. It was a perplexing sword that seemed to be rather attached to me, following me around and showing up whenever I really needed it. I'd unwittingly whet it with my blood, causing it to become even more attached to me.

Content that the mysterious angel sword had my back against the big bad vampire, I swept my arm out in an overly exaggerated welcoming gesture. "Then please, won't you come in."

The vampire bobbed his head in thanks, his blond curls voluminous and dancing around his head. I wondered what kind of shampoo he used because his hair was ah-mazing. He held his breath as he stepped over the threshold like he was expecting to spontaneously burst into flames or something. When he didn't become a fireball, I closed the door behind him.

"So, to what do I owe the pleasure of you showing up on my doorstep like a stray dog?" I asked, wandering into the kitchen. I pulled open the cutlery drawer and took out a wooden spoon. Shoving it handle-first into my knee brace, I groaned in relief as I scratched the itch that had been bothering me all day long.

I'd hurt it two weeks ago trying to find out who was making baby vampires. My shoulder—which I'd injured when my truck was hit by a semi, with me in it—had come out of the sling about a week ago. Aside from some stiffness, I was healing well.

The vampire's upper lip screwed up in distaste as I jettisoned the cooking utensil on the counter and shuffled toward the fridge.

"I'm going to pretend you used another simile."

I made a waving motion with my hand. "Go right ahead, but know that in here…" I tapped my temple with my index finger, "… I'm imagining you as a cute little teacup pug."

He actually growled at me. "My mistress sent me."

I paused as I reached for a bottle of water. Roxanne Monroe, mistress of the Buxton Vampire Kiss, was one of those supes who scared my extra pair of big girl pants off of me. "What does she want?"

Alistair slowly walked around my apartment, stopping to look at some of my ceramic unicorn statues on a shelf next to the

TV. Glancing at me over his shoulder, he pointed at a unicorn farting glitter and raised his eyebrows.

Huffing, I said, "What? Everyone needs a hobby."

"Yes, but I thought yours would've been guns or something."

"I much prefer wooden stakes and holy water."

Okay, yeah, that got me a glare. I shrugged. "What are you doing here because it sure as shit isn't to make fun of my collection."

"I didn't know about your collection," he replied smugly. "This is just a pleasant bonus."

I twisted the cap off my water and took a drink. "I'm sure it was. Look, can we just get down to it? I've had a long-ass day, I can't do kickboxing for another five and half months, and now I have a sulky vampire who showed up unannounced in my apartment."

"I'm not sulky."

"Petulant? Moody? Brooding? I could keep going."

The air seemed to chill then, the source of all that cold-and-unpleasant emanating from the pissed-off vampire across the room. "You'd best remember who you're talking to, Cat McKenzie."

I swallowed another mouthful of water, then mentally chastised myself. I'd just invited a vampire into my apartment and now I was antagonizing him. If that wasn't at the top of the list of dumb-ass moves, I didn't know what was. So, biting my tongue, I said, "I apologize. I'm not in a good mood. What is it that you came here to tell me?"

We had one of those Mexican standoffs then, only I had no hope of winning because as far as I knew, vampires didn't need to blink. With a resigned sigh, I replaced the cap on my bottle and leaned against the counter.

Reaching inside his jacket pocket, he produced a black business card on thick card stock and handed it to me. For a moment, I could only stare. I felt like I was on the cusp of falling down a rabbit hole—a rabbit hole filled with razor wire snares and poisonous walls…

But then I thought I was being paranoid.

It was just a bit of paper.

I took it, flipping it over and over, looking for a name or a number, but it appeared to be blank. I wondered what the gag was.

Alistair cleared his throat and said in an imperious voice, "Roxanne Monroe, Mistress of the Buxton Kiss is hereby in your debt, Catherine Ellen McKenzie."

I winced at the use of my full name.

"As such, you can speak the words 'Roxanne Monroe' three times to this card, and your desire for an audience with her will be relayed to the mistress."

I stared at the business card some more, then looked at him. "Seriously? Did you guys just rip off the *Beetlejuice* franchise?" He gave me a puzzled look. "Please tell me you've seen that movie?"

Alistair shook his head. "Human pop culture holds no interest for me."

I dropped the card onto the counter, then rocked back on my heels. "So, that's it?"

"That's it," he replied. "Welcome to the world of temporary-kiss protection."

"What happens after I use the card?"

"Then our association is done. Any goodwill you may have earned will be ended, and we'll be back to a relationship that only exists because Sawyer is a friend of the vampires."

"How *did* Sawyer become a friend of the vampires?"

The vampire gave me a smile that reminded me of a snake. "There are some things we don't discuss with outsiders."

"Outsiders?" I asked. "What, because I'm not a supe, I'm an outsider?"

"Precisely."

And with that, he turned on his designer shoes that matched his designer suit and strode to my front door. I glanced down at the card, touching the gilt-edge with my fingernail. It was like having a supernatural ace up the sleeve, and I would either never use it or covet the shit out of it.

I wondered how much I'd get for it on eBay.

A high-pitched whine suddenly filled the room, the resonance getting louder and louder with each second. When the glass in the windows began to shudder in their casements, I glanced at Alistair, who had stopped on the other side of the apartment door, his pale face stricken.

Before I could ask what was happening, the floor beneath my feet buckled, the building rocking from one side to the other.

Dust and debris fell onto my head, cracks appeared in the walls, but Alistair was still frozen to the spot. I looked to him, desperate for an explanation. I mean, he'd know, right? He was a centuries-old vampire.

I was knocked sideways when a boom went through the building. The sound of shattering glass echoed around me in surround sound, and my apartment building groaned like a dying beast. In the hallway, my neighbors began screaming and shouting, all running toward the stairs and down to the ground floor.

"What the hell?" I yelled over the noise. "Do you know what's going on?"

The vampire made a strangled sound, whispered, "Death magic," then *poofed* from the hallway.

I cursed as another shockwave went through the bricks, so strong that it knocked the air from my lungs. Looking down at my necklace, I found the opal my father had given me glowing brightly. The last time it had put on this kind of light show was back at Slayke when Sawyer and I had been bespelled, and we did things to each other no professional partners should.

Was that what was happening now? Was this magic?

The floor shuddered beneath my feet, a steady rhythm reminding me of an oncoming train. Some of my unicorn statues jumped off their shelves and smashed on the floor. Pictures swung violently on their hooks before finally being spewed off the wall too. I threw my hands over my ears when a high-pitched scream threatened to perforate my eardrums.

When the sound finally ebbed, my fingers came back sticky and wet with blood. Pocketing the card from Roxanne, I walked carefully to the door, leaving streaks of blood on the jamb as I peered into the hall. Outside, the walls were shaking like a nervous dog at the vet. The screams of the building's residents fleeing down the stairs surrounded me as I joined the frantic stream of people.

Jumping off on the floor below mine, I made my way to Sharyn Wyatt's apartment. The witch had helped with my last case, so if this was magic, she'd have to know something.

I walked as fast as my bum-knee would carry me, shuffling down the hall like a shambolic zombie in search of brains. Brains. Braaaiiinnnsss.

"Good Lord, what is that smell?" I covered my nose when the scent of sulfur became so thick it was almost visible. Then I was pulling at the collar of my sweater in an attempt to cool off. I looked up. Around.

Was there a fire on one of the other floors? I didn't smell any smoke…

Annnd then I saw a fireball shoot out of Sharyn Wyatt's open apartment door.

2

nother ball of flames came zooming out. It smashed into the hallway behind me, and I watched in horror as all the paint in a two-foot radius bubbled and peeled away.

What the fuck was that? Hellfire?

There was a squeak behind me, and I spun to see a young mother clutching a sleeping baby to her heaving chest. Her eyes darted from side to side, taking in the destruction.

"Run," I hissed. "Go!"

She bolted past me, stumbling and tripping when the floor buckled again. The shuddering made the marrow in my bones quiver and my teeth clack together. The woman fell to her knees with a curse, and I ran to her aid. With my hand under her arm, I managed to get the woman back on her feet and helped her into the stairwell, telling her to get her and the baby out of the building while she still could.

"Thank you," she gasped before disappearing down the stairs that were quickly filling with smoke.

I clutched at the shuddering walls, my bones rattling with each and every shimmy and shake of the Sheetrock. Making my way back to Sharyn's apartment, I cursed when I reached down for my sidearm and realized I didn't have it because I was an idiot, forgetting to pick it up on my mad dash out of my apartment. Reaver was mysteriously absent too.

Man, that sword and I were going to have a chat later.

With my back against the wall, I peered around the jamb, scanning the space efficiently before pulling back. There was one woman crouched down in the center of the living room, but it wasn't Sharyn. I took another look, sucking in a hiss when the scent of freshly spilled blood registered with my olfactory senses.

Maybe registered wasn't the right word.

It was more like they were drowning in a big vat of the stuff.

The woman began chanting, her words soft at first before the volume increased to a fever pitch. Magic rushed over me, and I shuddered as the sensation of a thousand spiders scrambled all over my skin. Against my chest, the opal began to pulse with heat.

I scratched at my arm and looked around for something I could use as a weapon. I spotted a wooden spoon that had been discarded by one of the building's residents in their mad dash to escape and snatched it up. It was insanity to run into that room with nothing but a wooden spoon, but as an officer of Buxton PD, it was my responsibility to go where nobody else wanted to go.

Like a spaceman…

A supernatural spaceman…

With a cooking utensil.

As if I needed the cosmic push, and a reminder that now was not the time to be thinking about my foray into space exploration, the opal around my neck kicked up its heat to nuclear.

"Right, let's do this."

I lurched into the room.

Then abruptly came to a stop.

Bile bit the back of my throat, my stomach sending the evac order as my brain tried to process what I was seeing, which was nothing but varying shades of red and chunks of things that should've been on the inside of a body.

Sharyn Flynn was prostrate, her mouth slack, her eyes clouded over in death. The other woman was crouched over the witch's body, her head bent as she worked a dagger into Sharyn's exposed stomach and chest. The woman was muttering something unintelligible while she worked. When the last word dripped from her lips, the wave of magic that hit me was like a sledgehammer, making my legs weak and my injured knee throb with my heartbeat.

Squeezing my eyes shut for a moment, I tried to breathe through my mouth, but the tang of blood lingered on the back of my tongue. When I reopened my eyes, I tightened my jaw and focused on what I needed to do.

Brandishing my not-so-lethal weapon, I cleared my throat "Buxton PD. Stop what you're doing."

Of course, my words would've had more impact if I wasn't holding a fucking spoon in front of me like it was a sword, but I was nothing if not resourceful. The woman turned to look at me through the curtain of her red hair, her muddy brown eyes small and spaced too closely together. Baring her white teeth at me, she hissed and stood. I had to crane my neck back as she did, judging her height to be somewhere at nearly the six-foot mark.

Man, I hated it when the bad guy was taller than me.

"Step away from the witch," I said, my voice holding steady despite the waver I felt in my throat. "And drop the weapon."

The woman did as I asked, moving away from Sharyn and dropping the knife. It clattered dully to the filthy, blood-and-gore-covered carpet. That was when I noticed the symbols that had been carved into Sharyn's body, each one of them flowing like water from one to another to another. There wasn't a single straightway or angle, the formation of those characters organic. I didn't recognize any of the markings, though—had never seen them before—but even looking at them, I knew they were magic, and it made my skin crawl.

Beside Sharyn was the body of a raven, its belly split open in a gross parody of what had happened to the witch. Bloody feathers were strewn around Sharyn's corpse, each feather's hollow shaft pointing inward toward the body.

With a hard swallow and mental ass-kicking to keep my shit together, I commanded, "Kick the knife toward me."

The woman smiled and did as I asked, and I shifted my eyes to the floor for a split second to check the trajectory of the blade—

The opal around my neck flared white-hot before blistering heat filled the room, making my head jerk up.

"Shit."

A fireball the size of a watermelon was coming at my chest. My body moved on instinct, and I found myself slamming onto the floor on my belly. The flaming ball went over my head, smaller flames sputtering onto the hardwood, into my hair, and onto my shoulders. With a curse, I patted out my smoldering clothes and hair before lumbering up onto my feet. My knee let out a holler as I got back on the vertical, and I could already hear Sawyer's voice in my head, chewing me out for rushing into the room without freaking backup.

A bolt of pain arced through my knee, the joint howling as I tried to put weight on it. Stumbling back against the small round dining table between the kitchen and me, I wiped the sweat from my brow, grit my teeth, and drew myself up. Fixing my gaze on the red-headed woman, I watched her stalk closer to me, mouthing words without sound. Extending out a hand, she reached for my chest…

No, not my chest.

My *necklace*.

I tried to lift my arm to ward her off, but my muscles locked, like a vice was suddenly banded around my chest, and my mouth was forcibly clamped shut. A strangled moan escaped my throat as she reached for the stone around my neck. Panic flared, the useless emotion doing nothing to help the current situation. The only thing that it made me do was zero in on one thought and one thought only—*I couldn't lose it.*

That necklace was the last thing my father had given me.

Struggling against the invisible hands that held me, a single tear leaked from the corner of one eye. But as her fingertips brushed the colorful stone, she was thrown across the room. The lock on my body disappeared as soon as she hit the couch, tipping the piece of furniture backward.

I looked down at the black opal around my neck.

Then at the couch that was flashing me what was under its skirt.

Well, *that* certainly hadn't happened before.

With a scream, the woman came to her feet, this time a ball of blue flames manifesting between her cupped palms.

Well, shit. Nothing good came from blue flames.

Tipping the small table over, I scrambled behind it just as she hurled the fireball at me, a cruel smile on her lips. My wooden shield blasted apart a second later, nothing but a shower of splinters and jagged pieces of timber forming a starburst on the hardwood. I looked up—

The opal pulsed once, propelling the blue fireball the woman had sent at me backward. She cursed and absorbed the blow like she was catching a football, the flames growing smaller and smaller until it was nothing but a wisp of smoke in the crook of her arm.

Screaming, she sent another fireball at me. Once again, my opal pulsed, and the fireball simply bounced off me and slammed into a wall. Again and again, volley after volley, she sent more fireballs at me, each one bouncing off and peppering the apartment with carnage.

The building rocked on its foundations from the onslaught, large chunks of the ceiling falling to the floor. The exposed brick walls were spidering with cracks at least an inch wide, exposing the steel bones of the apartment block. The floor vibrated beneath my feet, the plates and flatware in Sharyn's dish drainer rattling right along with it. The whole fucking building was going to go down, and I had no intention of being in there when it did.

I stared at the woman, torn between the need for justice and the pull of survival. I was leaning toward justice, though. I may not have liked Sharyn Wyatt, but she didn't deserve to die, and her murderer did not deserve to go free. Gritting my teeth, I opened my mouth to tell her to give it the fuck up when she slammed into me, tackling me to the ground.

Clearly, she'd given up on the idea of using magic.

Normally, that'd be fine by me.

But I essentially had one arm tied behind my back with my shoulder still bruised and hurting from the relocation of the joint. She rolled me over onto my back, then wrapped one hand around the chain of my necklace—being careful not to touch the stone—and began to yank on it. With my hands planted on her chest, I managed to shove her away once, but she simply lunged for my neck again, but just as she was about to wrap her hands around my throat, she began gasping for breath and fell away.

I stood, staring at her writhing around on the floor with clear oxygen deprivation issues. Movement near the front door caught my attention, and I turned to see a tall blond man standing between the jambs, the power oozing off him almost suffocating. He walked into the room, long hair tied loosely behind his head, exposing the sharpness of his cheekbones and the savagery of his pale green eyes. He reminded me of an arctic fox, his features angular and malicious.

I studied him warily—wearily—wondering what flavor of supe he was. He wasn't built like a shifter—those bastards were always stacked. Vampire maybe? No, his chest was heaving with his breath. He certainly dressed like a vampire, his designer suit probably costing more than three months' wage for me. Perhaps he was one of the fae? It seemed like the most plausible explanation.

His gaze shifted over to the woman, and he bared his sharp teeth.

"You bitch," he snarled, reaching for the other woman.

"She's my suspect, asshole," I gasped angrily, making him pause. "If anyone gets to rough her up, it's me."

His eyes darted to me, skimming my body with a sneer on his

lips. "You couldn't hardly harm a fly, *human.*"

"Maybe," I conceded. "But if you take her, you're interfering with a police investigation, and I'll have your ass in handcuffs faster than you can insult me again." Sawyer had once told me that the fae were sticklers for rules. Assuming this guy was one of the fae, playing the rule card now was a gamble I hoped paid off.

He studied me, his angry gaze sliding to the woman on the floor. She was still clutching her throat, her lips blue, her eyes bulging slightly as she gasped like a dying fish.

Using my strongest voice, I said, "Stop doing whatever it is you're doing to her and let the justice system do its job."

For a long minute, he stared at me.

For a long minute, I wondered whether I'd done the right thing by coming in between him and his target.

The thing was, I was a cop. It was my duty to make sure justice was served. With a small snarl, he flicked his hand toward the woman who sucked in a breath, gulping down the air like the supply would run out abruptly again.

"Who are you?" I demanded in a low voice, keeping an eye on the woman on the floor.

"Kailon Perry."

My eyes widened. I blinked.

And again…

…. one more for good luck.

"The fae assassin single-handedly responsible for revealing supernaturals to humans less than a year ago?"

He nodded and crossed his arms over his slender chest. "In the flesh."

Well, fuck.

3

"Cat?" Sawyer called from outside the ruined apartment.

"In here," I yelled back, my eyes still on Kailon. "What are you doing here?" I asked the fae softly.

Kailon's cool green eyes shifted down to the woman. "I'm here for her."

The color had returned to the woman's cheeks, her lips pink now instead of blue. She was still prostrate on the floor on account of me sitting on her chest to restrain her.

"Who is she anyway?"

Kailon's glamor fell away for a moment, revealing slitted acid green eyes, iridescent scaled skin, and a forked tongue.

Not an arctic fox—a snake, I realized.

"She's a witch, and she killed my niece last night."

"Why?"

"If I knew that—"

"McKenzie?" Sawyer yelled again. "Where are you?"

He was standing in the doorway to the apartment, his gaze scanning the ruined space. Couldn't he see us?

I looked to Kailon, his human packaging back in place once more. He flicked his hand, the air shimmering with a near physical wave. I knew the moment Sawyer could see us because his expression morphed from worry to anger. He barged into the room, shoving aside the broken and splintered furniture until he was standing nose to nose with Kailon.

"What's he doing here?" Sawyer demanded.

"Oh, this is too good." Kailon chuckled, taking a step back and flicking some debris from the lapel of his jacket.

Sawyer cocked his arm and slammed his fist into the fae's smug, smirking face. Kailon's head snapped violently to the side, a muffled *oomph* escaping his lips. Staggering backward, Kailon straightened slowly, wiping the back of his hand against his nose, smearing blood across his white cheek while Sawyer remained stock-still, his eyes violent black, his whole body rigid.

"Is that all you got?" Kailon baited with bared blood-stained teeth.

An animalistic sound bubbled from Sawyer's mouth just as a ripple of magic tingled against my skin. Sawyer slammed his fist into Kailon's face again, sending blood spraying. Not giving the fae a chance to recover, Sawyer drove Kailon's body right where I was sitting on the suspect.

I leaped up to avoid being crushed in the blur of fists and

blood, watching on helplessly. Behind me, the sound of crunching glass drew my attention, and I turned in time to see the witch diving through the broken living room window.

With a curse, I limped to it, my hands gripping the casement as I peered out onto the fire escape. The woman was racing down the stairs, her steps and movements almost like she was flying. I pulled my head back in and turned back to the brawling males.

"Well done, you… you… *assholes!*" I yelled. "She got away."

Whether it was my words or my generally shrill tone, the pair of them stopped trading punches long enough to stare at me. Blood was trickling from Sawyer's mouth, and along with a bloody nose, Kailon's eyebrow had been split open.

"Jesus!" I stalked into the galley kitchen—the only room that hadn't been hit by any stray fireballs.

Kailon staggered to his feet, brushing the dust and debris from his suit and straightening the jacket. Sawyer did the same, throwing a glare at Kailon and stepping toward me.

"What the hell happened here?" he demanded.

Now it was time for me to tread carefully.

Lying by omission was the name of the game, but I was a pro at playing.

"I was upstairs when the building began to rock from side to side, like it was an earthquake, except that we don't get earthquakes here. I ran downstairs, and I found the woman and Sharyn fighting with magic. She killed Sharyn, and that's when I tried to arrest her. She hurled some fireballs at me, then this guy showed up." I hiked my thumb in Kailon's direction. "He claims the woman who killed Sharyn also killed his niece, and he was about to tell me all about that when you came storming in like Mike Tyson ready to throw down."

Sawyer's eyes grew cold, the gray light that usually sparked in there flickering, guttering out. He swept his hand out angrily. "Do you even know who he is?"

I turned to glance at Kailon, who looked like a composed businessman there to discuss a potential partnership. "He's the fae responsible for shoving the supernatural world down everyone's throats. He's an assassin, and now I can add that his magical power is air manipulation."

"So you know he's dangerous."

I snorted and folded my arm under my brace. "Every goddamn supe is dangerous," I retorted. "I've just learned which ones are more dangerous than others."

Sawyer's eyes darkened, and he turned to Kailon. "Moira is dead?"

The fae nodded his head just once, challenge brimming in his eyes. "Yes."

"And what do you want us to do about it?"

"I want you to arrest the woman who did it."

"Why arrest her?" I asked. "You seemed pretty intent on killing her before I stopped you."

He studied me, his mouth curled up a little in the corner. "I was just trying to keep her quiet."

I snorted. "Is that what you call it?"

"Yes. The fae cannot lie," he replied.

"But they can twist the truth," Sawyer said in a clipped tone. His hands were cranked tightly into fists like he was ready to throw down again. "Why are you here?"

Kailon pressed his lips into a thin line before he leaned on the edge of the counter. "I've been hamstrung by the fae powers that be."

"What does that mean?"

Crossing one ankle over the other, he looked at me like he found me amusing. "It means that since my little stunt that revealed our existence, the most powerful fae have been keeping tabs on me. If I break any more laws, if I cause any more undue attention to be drawn to the supernatural community, I'll be killed. Publicly. As a warning to any other fae. Do you know much about public executions performed by the fae, Cat McKenzie?"

Kailon saying my name set me on edge for some reason. I shook my head. Dealing with supes was sooo-fucking-draining. "I'm not sure I have any fucks left to give here, but why don't you spill your secrets like a tween girl at a slumber party?"

He rolled his eyes. "I need this witch captured, and the only way I can do that is with your help. I can't break their decree not to hunt her."

"Why not?"

"Because the fae are bound by rules and laws, and because both heads of fae power don't want your government looking at us any more closely than they already have. You're the human police. I propose we make a deal. You arrest her, and after she's been contained and neutralized, the fae will take it from there."

"Wait." I looked at Sawyer, who was dabbing his split lip with a piece of kitchen towel, then looked back to the fae. "You want us to catch her *legally,* then hand her over to you and the fae to punish in whatever way you see fit?"

"Yes," he replied evenly.

Everything in me bucked against his request. The woman was a human. Sure, she'd pissed off the wrong people, but she was still a human.

Kailon said, "Think about it, and I'll be in touch, Cat McKenzie."

"I can't wait," I replied. Fuck. Why couldn't I catch a break?

Kailon walked from the room with all the confidence of a man who got everything he wanted in his long unnatural life.

Sawyer's hand on the small of my back made me jump, and I peered at him over my shoulder. "Are you okay?"

"How did you find out?" I asked, knocking bits of broken plate off the counter with the sweep of my arm. Easing myself onto the surface, I studied Sawyer's face. "And what's your beef with Kailon?"

He grimaced. "We have a history."

"Been putting your dick somewhere it doesn't belong?"

He shook his head, all innocent AF. "Not at all."

"What the f—"

I turned my head toward the door where Smith, an officer of Buxton PD, was standing.

He took in the carnage around the room. "Fucking hell, I thought out here looked bad." He shifted his gaze to me. "What happened in here?"

"Magic?" I answered absently, sliding off the counter. My knee buckled as I landed, and it was only Sawyer's hand on my elbow that stopped me from falling.

"Magic?" Smith repeated, sounding unconvinced.

I nodded. "Two witches. One fae. One bad-ass human." I cupped my hand like I was about to tell him a secret. "That was me, FYI."

He actually rolled his eyes at me.

Ooo, antagonism.

"You have a real high opinion of yourself, don't you, McKenzie?" Smith took another step into the room. I knew the moment he saw Sharyn's body because he came to a complete stop and rubbed a hand over his short hair. "Fuck."

"Mysterious witch, in the living room, with a dagger," I said.

Smith glared at me. "Have a little respect for the dead."

Turning to Sawyer, I muttered, "Some people have no appreciation for the classics."

My partner's expression was pissed off, but humor danced in his gray eyes. It was nice to see I hadn't lost my comedic value yet.

Smith came toward us, shooting a filthy look my way like I was the one who'd committed murder. "McKenzie, Wolfe will have your ass for this."

"For what? Living in the same building as a witch?"

The air thickened with tension, but it wasn't from me. Glancing over my shoulder, I saw Sawyer's eyes darken.

Smith bared his teeth. "Your fucking time is coming, McKenzie. You should stay with the freaks since nobody wants you back in the department anyway."

And with that declaration, he turned, stalked out of the kitchen, and continued into the hall.

"Well, someone got up on the wrong side of the bed."

Sawyer touched the small of my back, sending a shiver through me. "Smith is an asshole. Don't listen to him."

"I wasn't listening to him, Sawyer. I was playing with him. His fear of supes will eat him alive." I would know. It had almost happened to me not that long ago. "Hey, do me a favor and take a shot of the symbols on Sharyn's body before it's removed from the scene."

Sawyer did what I asked without question. Fucking miracle of miracles. He returned to me, angling the screen of his phone at me. I got the whole gruesome effect and gave him a tight nod.

"I've emailed them to you," he murmured.

Once the ME arrived, we wouldn't have been able to get close to the body and those symbols again until after the autopsy was done, and something told me we didn't have that kind of time.

Soon enough, the apartment was full of Buxton CSI, each person doing their thing while more officers stood just outside the door chatting to the emergency service workers who were checking all the apartments for any stragglers.

The building was empty now, the lack of structural integrity ensuring its residents wouldn't be returning.

"Let's head up to your apartment," Sawyer suggested, leading the way up the broken and cracked concrete stairs and onto the floor above. A firefighter still lingering on my floor let Sawyer help me to my apartment, so I could collect some things before I was officially made homeless too.

I sucked in a breath when I saw my place. It was a mess. Everything that had been on the walls was no longer there. Dust, Sheetrock, broken dishes and glass littered the floor. I picked up one half of my rainbow farting unicorn statue that hadn't been smashed into a thousand pieces and looked at it.

"Go and pack a bag, pussy cat," Sawyer said.

I turned to him, tears sitting unshed in my eyes. "Where am I supposed to go? I can't afford to stay at a hotel until this place is repaired."

"My place," he replied firmly. He looked around at the damage. "And I doubt this apartment block will be rebuilt. There's been too much structural damage done."

I wasn't sure why, but that declaration made me sad. This was *my* place, the only place I'd ever had. I loved everything about it. Still, I nodded and hobbled into the bedroom. Pulling a bag from the closet, I filled it with clothes, then took down another to salvage some of my unicorn collection that hadn't been decimated in the destruction.

As soon as I stepped out of my room, Sawyer was there, taking the bag from my hand.

"Only one bag?"

I sniffled. "There's another one on my bed."

Handing me my phone, which had somehow not been destroyed in the process of being left in my apartment, he ducked back into my bedroom.

"How's the knee? I noticed you were limping before," he said when he came back out.

Grunting, I replied, "I hope I haven't done any more damage to it by playing superhero."

He shuffled the bags to just one of his hands, so he could slide his free arm around my waist. I leaned against him as he led me from the apartment.

After picking our way through the debris, we finally made it outside, walking past everyone who had gotten out, a crowd of gawking people and emergency service workers. If it were under any other circumstances, I would've been ogling the shit out of them all because firemen are yummy.

"Are you thinking about the nice policeman in uniform, pussy cat?" Sawyer asked into my ear, a teasing growl in his voice.

I gave him the stink eye. Having an incubus for a partner sucked sometimes. "It was the fireman, if you must know."

"I don't think you're in any state to try and seduce someone."

"I don't want seduction, Sawyer. I'd just imitate a starfish and let them have at it."

A wave of lust shot through me as my words affected my partner. Being an incubus, he fed off sexual energy and was able to manipulate sexual feelings—sexual feelings I had for him in spades. I'd had a taste of Sawyer, and even though I shouldn't want more, I did.

I moaned, "Can you please stop?"

"Stop what?"

"You're doing that thing again." I waved my hand in the general direction of his crotch. "The thing we don't talk about anymore."

"The thing *you* don't want to talk about, you mean." At my eye roll, he added, "We'll have to talk about what happened at Slayke sooner or later."

What happened at Slayke was something I'd thought about nonstop in private. We'd been bespelled. Sawyer had given me three orgasms on the dancefloor before the haze of lust had lifted for me. Sawyer, being the incubus he was, hadn't gotten off so lightly—*no pun intended*. He'd been dragged into a sexual frenzy where he screwed multiple women against the walls for hours, and only stopped when the owners of the club had knocked him out cold.

I knew he still felt guilty for what had happened.

"No, I don't."

He cursed under his breath, and like a switch had been flipped, the sensation of wanting to dry hump his leg suddenly went away. Blowing the hair from my face, I glared at him. "Dick."

"You were the one who mentioned it first."

Oh, yeah, I totally was.

"Cat, do you think we'll ever talk about—"

"No, thank you," I replied quickly, cutting him off. No, I didn't want to rehash what happened at Slayke. I wanted to put that little incident far back into my mind and only bring it out in private moments.

He muttered something about being stubborn but didn't push the issue. When we arrived at my truck, he helped me in, threw my bags into the back then got into the driver's side. Thank fuck that hadn't been damaged by falling debris. I only got it yesterday after having to replace the other one after our unfortunate vampire-related accident two weeks ago.

Seriously, how was this my life now?

"How did you get here?"

"My motorcycle," he said. "I'll get it tomorrow."

On the drive to his place, we didn't talk, mostly because I was contemplating how I was going to get my hands on more unicorn statues. I was definitely going to be hitting up Amazon when I got to his place. I looked at Sawyer from the corner of my eye. I wondered if he'd store all my awesome new unicorn purchases when they arrived.

Finally, sick of the silence, I sighed. "I hope you have lots of storage space. At least an empty closet I can use. Maybe a shit ton of Tupperware? Storage locker?"

His gaze flickered over to me briefly before returning to the road. "Why would I need lots of storage?"

"Why?" I asked, outraged. "For all the unicorn statues I'll be getting delivered to your place while I look for somewhere else to live."

He arched a brow, then slowly ran his fingertips along the sweep of the steering wheel as he thought. "You're buying more unicorn statues?"

I jerked my head around to face him, my mouth popping open. "After that destruction, why wouldn't I get more?"

Shaking his head, he said, "I don't even know where to begin answering that."

I snorted. "Start by saying you have available storage at your place."

I took his silence as agreement.

"I don't even know where you live."

"And why would you?"

"I don't know. We're partners. You know where I live… correction, *lived*."

He shook his head after a minute, clearly having undergone some sort of silent conversation with himself that I had nothing to do with. "I live in the Astoria Building."

I whistled through my teeth. "That new one on 5th?" At his nod, I added, "Who knew Buxton PD paid so well." I knew that wasn't it. I'd found out he was pretty old—like 1860s old—so being loaded seemed to be a thing these supes had going for them.

"Well, I hope you have Netflix because I have a list as long as my arm of all the shows I want to binge." He gave me a sideways glance before returning his eyes to the road. "Like chick flicks."

I smiled when I heard him groan.

He finally slowed my truck in front of his building, reversing into a spot that had just freed up. Looking out the window,

I stared up at the Astoria Building. It was a forty-plus story building made of steel and glass.

"Which one is yours?" I asked, gesturing to the behemoth on the other side of the street.

He bobbed down and pointed about two-thirds of the way up the structure. "Thirty-third floor."

I opened my door. "So, you actually have room for me here?"

"I have a spare room that you can use for as long as you need."

"Does it come with a wake-up call?"

I grinned at the flat stare he gave me. "This isn't a hotel, Cat."

We walked into the lobby, greeting the doorman as we did. The lobby was filled with white marble floors and off-white walls. Recessed lighting spotlit expensive artworks on the walls and objects d'art carefully displayed in niches.

I whistled through my teeth. "How much was this place?"

"Enough," he replied simply, reaching for the elevator button. The up arrow lit, and we waited.

"Thank you for taking me in."

"What are partners for?"

The elevator arrived and we got inside, riding the thirty-three floors up to his apartment. When the car slowed to a stop and opened with a pleasant *ding!*, I followed him to the door. When I stepped inside, I found his personal space was filled with warm woods and taupe furniture. His place was about triple the size my apartment had been with a large gourmet kitchen, an even larger living room and a hallway that led into even more rooms.

"You must be exhausted," he said. "Do you want to go straight to bed, or would you like to eat first?"

God, how long had it been since I'd eaten?

"Food, please."

He gave me a tight nod and walked us toward the giant stainless-steel and black marble kitchen. Depositing me on a stool, he walked into the galley kitchen and ran a dish towel under the tap. He tossed the cloth to me and nodded at my hands.

I glanced down. Right. Covered in blood.

While I got busy cleaning my hands, he pulled open the fridge and began rummaging through until he found what he was looking for. I watched him throw together a couple of sandwiches, adding a handful of chips on the side.

I grinned at him. "Mrs. Brown used to do that, too," I told him, munching on a chip.

"You can't have a sandwich without them," he replied, taking a bite of his own meal. "How are you feeling? How's the knee? Can I get you anything?"

"I couldn't get into my bathroom to get the pain meds," I said. "Would you be able to get some more from the drug store?"

"Sure. I'll go after dinner."

I nodded. "Thank you." We ate together in silence, and for once, I had nothing funny to say, no amusing observations that I knew Sawyer enjoyed hearing. I blamed it on the wave of exhaustion suddenly crashing over me.

"Are you sure you don't want to go and get your knee looked

at in the hospital?"

"No, it's fine."

"I really think you should."

I stared at him. "If it gets any worse, I'll go to the hospital. Promise."

Sawyer seemed to be happy enough with that answer because he went back to eating. Meanwhile, I was struggling against the tide of exhaustion that was threatening to take over. Propping my head in my hand, I watched him for a moment…

"Cat? Wake up."

"Hmm?" I mumbled, wiping my gritty eyes. I could barely open them, but when I did, I got an up-close-and-personal of Sawyer's painfully handsome face. He was staring at me with such concern, his gray eyes soft and tender.

"Come on. Let's get you to bed."

"Bed…" Yeah, that sounded pretty good. He helped me stand, leading me down in a shuffle to a guest bedroom.

"Stay there, and I'll get you changed."

Changed? No, I didn't need help with that. Blindly, I swatted away his hands as he undid the buttons on my jeans.

"Shh, Cat, let me help you." Sawyer gently moved my hands out of the way.

"Fine, but don't stare at any of my fun-zones for more than two seconds," I grouched in a sleep-heavy slur.

His chuckle was warm and comforting in my ear. "Even semi-conscious…" His words turned muffled, and although I wanted to demand what he was thinking, my mouth was clamped shut, my brain shutting down and sliding into REM land.

I jerked back into awareness when Sawyer slid my foot through the leg of my jeans. "Don't forget the card," I mumbled incoherently.

"What card?" he whispered.

I frowned. "The one in my back pock—"

4

I woke with a start, trying to figure out where I was and who I was with. I didn't wake up in random people's bedrooms all that often, but if I *had* had sex last night, it was super unmemorable.

Sucked to be that guy.

I turned my head when I heard someone banging around in the room beyond, then my gaze dropped to my bags set against the wall.

Sawyer's apartment.

That's where I was.

Rubbing my face, I threw off the blanket that had been laid across my body and…

Gone were my filthy, blood-soaked clothes from last night, and in their place were my cute pajamas featuring unicorns carrying submachine guns. Sure, they were a little unbelievable—I mean, everyone knew unicorns preferred grenade launchers—but I didn't discriminate when it came to unicorns.

Ever.

I got a flash of a memory.

Sawyer removing my pants gently.

Me telling him to avert his eyes…

Him chuckling…

Shaking my head, I told myself I could be embarrassed later. Slowly, I sat up and slid off the edge of the mattress. When I stood, I prepared for a flash of pain to shoot through my unbraced knee. I looked down when there wasn't even a twinge. In fact, even the bruising had faded along with the swelling. Bending my knee a few times, I tested it.

No pain.

No spasms.

No aches.

It was like the bone bruise had never happened.

"How's it feeling?" Sawyer asked.

I glanced up to find him leaning against the door, two mugs of coffee in his hands. Pushing off the jamb, he strolled toward me, handing a mug to me.

I took a sip then replied, "Brand new. But how?"

He ducked his eyes. "I called in a favor."

"A favor from who?"

"Don't you mean from *whom*?"

"Don't correct my grammar. Tell me who healed me."

Lowering himself onto the edge of my bed, he looked down into his coffee cup. "A gnome."

"Like what you find in the garden?"

Shaking his head, he said, "No, not like that at all." He rubbed his eyes with his thumb and forefinger like talking to me was exhausting. "Look, your knee is healed now. Can we just leave it at that?"

I studied his face. "Why?"

"Because I asked him to."

"No, not that. Why did you use your favor for me?"

"Because I don't like to see you in pain." Sawyer's gaze became remote, like he was trying to shut a door on his emotions. "Who gave you that card?"

I blinked, thrown by the change of subject. "What card?"

"The one I took out of your back pocket last night," he prompted. "The black one on the bureau."

Oh, that card.

Running my fingers over the rim of my mug, I murmured, "Alistair came to see me before everything went down."

His brows rose. "Did he? How did he know where you lived?"

I shrugged. I didn't want to particularly think of that either. Just having the vampire in my apartment had been enough of a mind-fuck. "No clue, but he was waiting at my door after my therapist appointment yesterday afternoon."

"What did he say?"

I stood, marveling at the complete lack of pain, and walked over to the bureau to pick up the heavy-stock business card. Flipping it over and over again in my fingers, the gilt edges winked with each revolution. "He told me I was under the protection of the kiss, that all I had to do was say the mistress's name three times when I was ready to call in that favor."

When he stayed quiet, I stared at him. That remote expression hadn't shifted from his face, and the fact that it hadn't made my heart pound.

"Just say it."

"What?"

"Tell me what bad juju this is." Steeling myself with a sip of caffeine, I asked, "What have I gotten myself into now?"

He shook his head. "I don't know. I've never heard of the kiss extending protection to anyone like this before."

"Oh, great! So I'm the guinea pig for vampires now? Seriously?"

"It'll be fine, Cat."

Narrowing my eyes at him, I said, "Not making me feel any better here. If anything, I can add *scared out of my pants* to my already full dance card of *pissed off, a feeling of impending doom,* and *crippling anxiety.*"

LATER THAT DAY, I COLLAPSED ONTO THE OTHER SIDE OF THE couch Sawyer was sitting on. My mind was fried after spending the afternoon researching the symbols that had been carved into Sharyn's body and getting absolutely nowhere. I'd followed link after link, breadcrumb after breadcrumb until my head was full of signs, ideograms and hieroglyphics.

There had been a couple of possible explanations for the markings I'd seen, but neither of them truly fit since there were slight differences between the ones I'd seen online and the ones Sawyer had snapped on his phone.

Perhaps I needed a more direct source. My first thought had been Kailon, but I was wary of asking the fae. I didn't want to owe him anything. Being indebted to a fae could lead me to being obliged to hand over anything from a cheeseburger to my first-born child.

Passing me a beer, Sawyer took a sip of his own drink and swallowed. "Find anything?"

"Nada. You?"

He shook his head. On the table in front of him were open books stacked one on top of the other along with a pad of paper that had doodles of the symbols on it.

"Got any witches on your payroll?" I asked off-handedly.

"I've already called her. We're meeting her first thing Monday morning."

"Really? I was kind of joking. Can we trust her?"

"Yeah, we can. She's been officially and unofficially helping me with cases for a few years now."

"Who is she?" I took a long pull from my beer.

"Her name is Amy Elliot. She's been practicing in Buxton for the past twenty years."

"And if she can't help us?"

He pursed his lips into a hard line and inhaled sharply through his nose. "I don't know."

"What about Kailon?" I studied his face, watching it morph from relaxed to enraged in a nanosecond.

"What about that motherfucker?" he asked through his gritted teeth.

"I know owing a fae is a no-no, but he's already asked something of us. Shouldn't we be able to do the same?"

"Technically, yes, but I would no sooner trust him than a rabid dog not to bite. But you need to be careful when it comes to the fae, Cat."

I slid my legs beneath my body and turned to him. "What's your beef with him anyway?" Sawyer didn't say anything for a long minute, so I glanced over at him. "If it's something that's going to affect this case, I need to know."

"I don't see why you'd need to know. I can keep my personal shit to myself on a case."

My brows rose. "Really? Yeah, I guess that's what your brawl in Sharyn's apartment was… you know the one where you let the suspect escape. Yep, that was you keeping your personal shit locked up tight."

He rolled his eyes at my sarcasm. "Just drop it, McKenzie."

McKenzie? Oh, I'd hit a nerve. Perfect. "Tell me, Sawyer, or are you too chicken shit?"

He let out a low growl. "I tell you what, I'll make you a deal. I tell you if you talk to me about what happened at Slayke."

I blinked. "Why? We already discussed it at the hospital after I killed Draco," I hedged. Draco was the vampire who'd killed my father in retribution for destroying his kiss twelve years earlier.

"No, you blew me off and changed the subject."

I frowned. So, yeah, okay, I had done that, but I don't do feelings and talking about how much I wanted my partner—my *incubus* partner—to follow up those three *a-ma-zing* orgasms from the club just wasn't something I wanted to give airtime.

Instead of being a grown-up about the whole thing, I told him, "Forgive me if I don't want to rehash what happened in that club." The truth of the matter was that I'd wanted more—*still* wanted more.

But wanting more would ruin everything Sawyer and I had going on.

Unwilling to fall down this rabbit hole of a conversation, I hauled myself onto my feet and walked into the kitchen to get a glass of water. I paused, however, when I heard a car alarm go off outside.

Then another.

And another.

Racing to the window, I pressed my nose to the glass and peered down onto the street.

"Mother*fucker!*"

5

I ran out of the apartment, chanting three words I never thought I'd have to say again. "Not my truck. Not my truck. Not my *fucking new* truck."

Punching the button on the elevator, Sawyer appeared at my side.

"What was—"

"You don't want to know the answer," he replied, his jaw tight, his eyes darkening.

When the elevator arrived with a *ding*, we stepped into the car and hit the button for the lobby.

"What's that doing here?" I muttered, picking up Reaver who was propped up in the corner like it had been waiting for us.

"At least it showed up," Sawyer replied. "Keep it with you."

The whole ride down, the walls shivered every few seconds,

making me hold onto the railing to steady myself.

The elevator slowed to a stop. The doors opened slowly, revealing a group of panicked people rushing to get in. Shoving our way free, we hurried to the front door of the building, lurching when the floor buckled and bowed.

"You know, I'm starting to think I'm cursed here," I said to Sawyer as I gripped the arm he'd thrown out to stop me from falling. At his raised brows, I added, "You know, with buildings falling apart around me."

The floor shook again, the reverberations slamming into my joints and making my teeth rattle.

"Come on."

A man raced through the front door then, the look of absolute terror giving me pause. If he was scared, I then knew what I'd seen from the window had been real. I watched him run to the bank of elevators, pressing the call button like his life depended on it.

Rushing outside, I used the wall for support as another shockwave went through me. The ripples were rhythmic, like those of something heavy walking on a hardwood floor. Sawyer had lowered his center of gravity, his knees bent, riding every aftershock. The sidewalk ahead of me had cracked, each fissure slowly inching apart with each vibration.

I looked up to find two hairy, three-toed feet the size of city buses in length coming toward me. As I let my gaze drift up, I saw what those feet were connected to and wished we hadn't bothered coming to investigate.

At least sixty-five feet in the air above me stood a green-furred creature that would've looked like a man if it weren't for his three-fingered hands. All the other features looked too small for the dimensions of its face—the green eyes piggish and too close together, the nose bulbous. Pointed bat-like ears topped off the ugly ensemble—and then there was its flaccid sex hanging between its legs, its testicles the size of tractor tires.

Looking over, I saw what few people who were on the street had now gone, all finding safety. Well, bully for them. And with no other police yet on the scene, it looked like it was up to us.

Holding Reaver out in front of me, I demanded, "Sawyer, what is that?"

"It's a gremlin."

I blinked at him as my fear morphed into irrational anger. "All my childhood impressions of gremlins are now ruined!" I yelled at him.

I didn't know why I was yelling.

Oh, yes I did.

It was better than curling into a ball and crying in the corner, which was looking like a more appealing option.

"I told you they were big." He took out his phone and hit a number on speed dial. "Yeah, we need backup. Bull gremlin on the loose outside the Astoria Building on 5th."

"What can we do?" I glanced up at the windows of the apartments on either side of the street. Frightened faces were pressed against the glass, their curiosity fighting with their fear. "There's a lot of collateral damage potential here."

Sawyer followed my gaze and nodded.

I turned when the sound of screaming, twisting metal and shattering glass reached me. The gremlin had just stomped its bus-sized, hairy feet down on my brand new truck. "No!" I yelled, my arms outstretched in front of me like that would stop the destruction. "Not my new truck!"

The gremlin smiled at me revealing yellowing, broken teeth and ground its heel down even harder. I was going to punch the bastard in the balls for that. Spinning, I demanded frantically, "How do we stop him?" I gestured wildly at the gremlin who had scooped up my truck and was holding it in its furry hand, plucking off the wheels as the alarm system slowly died to a squeak.

"We can't do anything until we get backup," he replied calmly.

I turned back to watch the final shuddering breaths of my new truck, cursing the bastard who crushed it. "Please tell me they'll bring some awesome weapon to stop it," I whined.

"They will," Sawyer replied. "All we can do now is wait."

Wait and watch my truck get eaten because that's what the fucking gremlin was doing now. Chewing on the bed, metal screeched and groaned between his giant jaws. How in the hell was I supposed to pay for another truck? Insurance barely came to the party with the last accident. Somehow, I didn't think 'consumed by a green gremlin' was going to be a sufficient reason this time.

"What can we do while we wait for backup?"

"There's nothing to do, Cat. This fucker is as tall as a six-story building. I don't know what you expect to do."

Flipping him off mentally, I scanned the street. Why was the big hairy bastard not targeting anyone else's cars? "Where did it come from? Maybe we can lure it back there."

"Wonderland," my partner said, and I fought the shiver that tracked up each and every one of my vertebrae. Wonderland was what the humans and other supernatural creatures called the domain of the fae. A weird parallel universe, it mirrored our world—from what I'd *accidentally* seen anyway—only everything over there could kill you without a second thought.

I didn't want to go back there. Technically, I shouldn't have been able to go in there in the first place, but I was a special cupcake—apparently.

"Should we at least try to take it in the direction of the docks then?" I'd unwittingly stumbled into Wonderland the last time we were investigating a crime down there. I hadn't known at the time where I was or who I'd encountered, but it was enough for me to know that I didn't want a repeat performance.

Sawyer stared at me like I'd lost my mind. "The entrance to Wonderland isn't always in the same place. It changes according to the will of the current Sidhe Queen."

I held my hands up in front of me, imploring him to stop. I hated how he just kept dropping information on me like that. It was like he was waiting for the moment where there'd be maximum freak-out time, then…

BOOM!

Supernatural truth bomb.

"Why?" I whined. "Why must the supernatural thing always be so freaking hard? And wipe that smirk off your face, Sawyer Taylor, or I'm going to become the roommate from hell." When he said nothing, I asked, "Do you know where the entrance is now?"

"No."

"Could it still be down at the docks?"

He shrugged.

I turned around when I realized I hadn't been able to hear the tragic melody of screaming metal on enamel. Really, my observational skills could do with some work because by the way the gremlin was frozen to the spot with its mouth gaping, it had been a while. Its green lips were turning blue, a sure sign that hypoxia was the name of the game. Held weakly in its furred hand was my mangled truck—well, what was left of my mangled truck. Three wheels were gone. The last remaining survivor was worse for wear—hanging off at a cock-eyed angle.

I scanned the street again, squinting when I saw the shadows move in the alleyway across the road.

That's when I saw Kailon Perry emerge.

"I thought you could do with some help to slow it down," the fae rumbled in his smooth, glassy voice.

"We don't need your help," Sawyer replied in a dangerous drawl.

Kailon was unruffled by Sawyer's hostility. "I think you're wrong about that." He was dressed in another suit, this one black on black on black—black suit, black shirt, black tie. His gaze narrowed on Reaver. "That's a very interesting sword, Cat

McKenzie."

Instinctively, I moved my arm holding the sword behind my back. "Are you going to kill it?" I asked Kailon, flicking my free hand in the direction of the gremlin.

"I could if that's what you wanted." Such dark promises in his words.

"Cat," Sawyer warned. I turned to look at him. "Be careful."

"She has nothing to fear from me," Kailon purred, flicking Sawyer an annoyed glare. "Do you, Cat?"

Shaking my head because I'd had just about enough of the fae, I snapped, "Cut the shit. Why are you here, Kailon?"

"Excuse me?" he asked, pretending to be affronted by the question.

"How did you know to come here now? Why are you helping us? To prove to us you can be useful?"

"No."

"Did you send the gremlin?"

He gave an ophidian smile. "Why would I set a gremlin loose in downtown Buxton? They're lumbering idiots who have brains the size of walnuts."

"Because you want to make a point."

"And that point is?"

"That you can send anything our way if we don't catch this witch for you."

His brows hiked into his hairline. "It's a wonder you made it this far in life without trusting people," he murmured.

"Oh, I did trust people, but it turned out everything I was told is a lie." Starting with my parents and birth. Apparently, I was the culmination of two of the strongest bloodlines of Rogue Faction—a clandestine group who hunted supes before the supes had even come out of the closet. And the only person who truly knew anything about me was Mrs. Brown, the elderly woman who had practically raised me when my dad went AWOL after my mother's death.

Kailon narrowed his green eyes at me. "I have a penthouse suite a couple of buildings away, Cat. I sensed the gremlin was coming, and I came to see if I could help."

Call me stupid, but I believed him. My opal lay quietly against my heart, the fact that it wasn't reacting giving me all the evidence I needed. If Kailon was manipulating the situation, I had no doubt the opal would've lit up like a Christmas tree.

The gremlin made a sharp, keening noise, and I looked up to find its green eyes on Kailon. He knew the fae had the power to control his air flow.

"I'd rather you didn't kill it," I said. Unnecessary cruelty wasn't something I delighted in. "But we need to… I don't know, knock it out so we can remove it from downtown."

He stared at me for a beat, stared with an intensity that made me shift on my feet. "I will do this for you *if*…" I braced myself for the words 'if you let me kill the witch,' so color me surprised when he finished with, "… you agree to come out to dinner with me."

"McKenzie!" Sawyer barked, drawing my attention. He shook his head, the muscles in his jaw feathering. I frowned. Was he telling me no so I wouldn't get involved with him, or no because Kailon was dangerous? I already knew he was dangerous, but so was a six-story gremlin on the loose downtown.

Returning my eyes to Kailon, I had a fleeting thought that I was doing the wrong thing, but then again, what other choice did I have? "Fine," I bit out. "Dinner only." I looked up at the gremlin. "Knock him out."

The fae sketched a bow and blew in the direction of the gremlin. The creature's limbs went limp, his nobby knees falling out from under him. When it slammed into the road, its boar-coarse fur sounded like the bristles of a stiff broom hitting a tile floor. The asphalt cracked beneath it, sending the cars that lined the street airborne for a moment before slamming back down to earth.

I opened my mouth to thank the fae but shut it at the last minute. I didn't want to be indebted to the bastard. Being held to a date was bad enough.

AN HOUR LATER, I—ALONG WITH ABOUT A HUNDRED OTHER PEOPLE who had come down for the show now that the danger was over—watched three tow trucks haul the unconscious gremlin away, its green fur buffeting the parked cars as it went. They rocked on their tires, the suspension picking up the slack as the giant metal bodies resettled like a bunch of birds ruffling their feathers.

"Where will they take it?" I asked Sawyer, who stood beside me.

"Out of the city limits, somewhere like a field where it can wake up slowly."

"Will it come back?"

He shook his head. "I don't think so. Gremlins don't have large brains, so complex thoughts about terrorizing a city just aren't in there unless someone put them there."

"You think someone sent it here on purpose?"

"Maybe. Yes." He finally turned his stormy eyes to me. "I also think that's why only your truck was targeted."

I looked around the street. He was right. None of the other cars had been touched. Their alarms had only been set off on its arrival into the city because it was stomping around.

I wanted to scream, but I held my frustration back. "Why is it always me?"

A small smirk formed on his perfect mouth. "You do seem to draw the supes to you."

"Argh, don't be a bag of dicks." I looked over at my crushed truck. All four tires were now gone thanks to the six-story drop. The tray had been masticated like a pit bull's chew toy, so it was less than three-quarters of what it used to be, the hood and roof had been dented into the shape of a gremlin hand and every single window had been shattered. "My truck," I whimpered.

Sawyer drew his arm around my shoulders and turned us back to his apartment building. The regular cops had cordoned off the scene and shut down the road in both directions while they worked to remove the gremlin, and the yellow tape was like a beacon for onlookers. Every man and his dog were standing as close to the line as they could get, their phones out either taking photos or recording what had happened.

We ducked under the tape and pushed through the crowd. All I wanted to do was go to bed. The last couple of days had finally topped off my I-can't-handle-any-more-shit bucket.

Back in the apartment, Sawyer announced that he'd make me some tea while I took a shower. Unwilling to argue that I didn't actually *like* tea, I shuffled off into the bathroom, depositing Reaver on top of the bureau as I passed through the bedroom. Undressing quickly, I moaned as soon as I set foot under the spray. It was so good, and I needed the hot water to wash everything away. I had just turned around to rinse out the shampoo I'd been rubbing into my hair when I yelped. Sawyer was leaning against the counter, his eyes unreadable.

I covered myself with my arms and hands, then demanded, "What the hell, Sawyer? I think this goes beyond what partners do together."

"I've seen you naked before," he said matter-of-factly.

I tried not to roll my eyes. Yes, he had seen me naked before—after my numerous trips to the hospital, but most recently last night after passing out from exhaustion. "That was different. I was almost completely incapacitated in every other instance then."

He didn't say anything to that, nor did he move. He just watched me with an intense expression. I felt like he was sliding back into asshole-Sawyer mode like when I'd first met him. I didn't want him to go back to that. I needed him to be the guy who laughed at my jokes—because, hello, I'm hilarious—but also the guy who backed me the fuck up.

When he didn't move or say anything for a good minute, I rinsed out the remaining shampoo. If he wanted to stand there, he could knock himself out, but I was going to get what I needed done. Squirting some conditioner into my hand, I ran it through the tips of my hair then set about washing myself.

I yelped again when Sawyer finally spoke. "I don't want you to have dinner with Kailon."

Rubbing the steam from the glass shower screen, I glared at him. "It's dinner. We're not getting married."

"I don't trust him."

Well, that made two of us.

"He stopped that gremlin for us without anyone else getting injured. All he's asked in return was to go out to dinner with me. It's actually a great opportunity to question him."

"I don't like it." The words were practically thrown at me.

Tipping my head back, I kept my eyes on Sawyer as I rinsed out the conditioner. "Why not?"

He balled his hands into fists. "Because I don't like the way he looks at you," he all but roared, his mask of civility dropping for a second.

I blinked. "The way he… Oh, my God! You're jealous!" I crowed, shutting off the water. "You're jealous that another man is interested in me."

He folded his arms defiantly. "That's not it at all."

"And I'm calling bullshit." I squeezed the water from my hair.

With a growl, he yanked open the shower door and stepped inside. He tilted my chin up, making me look into his eyes. They were roiling like molten mercury, the intensity of his expression making me squirm. "Is that what you want to hear? That I'm jealous? Because I *fucking* am."

All the air in my body left in a rush. "What?" I whispered, hating how vulnerable I sounded.

"I want you more than I want my next breath, Cat… just like you want me."

The need to deny my feelings rose until I felt as if I was choking on them. And honestly, the strength of them frightened me. I had no idea whether what I was feeling was real, or if it was Sawyer manipulating my emotions. All I knew was that something had been awakened in me that night in Slayke.

Tentatively reaching for me, he stroked my cheek with his thumb. "Look at your necklace and know that I'm not influencing you right now." His voice was as smooth as velvet and as dangerous as shattered glass.

I looked down and saw the black opal was quiet against my chest.

"But we can't give in to this," he whispered, leaning in and kissing the corner of my mouth. "We can't. It's madness to even entertain the idea of acting on these feelings, but Cat… Jesus, I've never felt this before."

"What?" I rasped.

"Like I want *more*." He dropped another kiss onto the side of my neck this time, his tongue sliding up my throat while an erotic purring filled the shower.

"I want more, too," I whispered, clinging to his shoulders, feeling the heat beading off his body. Squeezing my eyes shut, I breathed through the stab of lust that was assaulting my body. Inside my chest, my heart pounded against my ribs as I stepped out of his hold and backed myself against the shower wall. He was right, of course. We couldn't do this, couldn't stumble and fall over the line. But why did it have to hurt so much?

The tile was cold against my skin—the perfect match to the freezing ache in my chest. "I need to get dressed."

Hurt flickered in his eyes, and I met that pain head-on. I needed to remind myself that sex—no matter how amazing it would be—wasn't worth losing my partner over. Seeing him with other women, or the aftermath of being with another woman, would *kill* me. Panting through my open mouth, I silently begged him to go. Having him this close—having him showing me the raw truth—was torture.

Clearly, he read that in my eyes because after one final nod, he opened the shower door and stepped out, leaving a trail of wet footsteps in his wake.

6

I avoided Sawyer for the rest of the weekend. His admission was everything I wanted to hear and everything I was terrified to learn. A relationship with an incubus would be nothing but heartbreak, of that I was sure. I wondered if he was even capable of love—real love—or whether something in his biology prevented it. I mean, he needed to feed like I needed to breathe, except my respiration didn't depend on an orgasm inside a female.

Monogamy just wasn't possible, so there really was no point, was there?

I'd just finished making myself a cup of coffee on Monday morning when Sawyer strolled into the kitchen wearing his black slacks and black dress shirt, the damn fabric clinging to his shoulders and chest. Across his broad torso was a black nylon and Velcro holster, its thick straps straining against his pectoral muscles. Tucked under his left arm was his department-issued Glock 22, the butt of the gun sitting snug under his armpit.

My own Glock was looking far less menacing in an identical holster across my chest.

"Good morning," he said, reaching around me for a cup and the coffee pot. His whisky and chocolate scent shot straight between my legs, and I stepped to the side, giving him a wide berth. The bastard could smell lust like a shark could smell blood in the water.

"Morning." Pressing my back against the granite counter, I asked, "What time are we meeting the witch?"

"Nine o'clock at her work."

"And where's her work?"

He turned around, slowly stirring his coffee. I didn't know why, but I noticed how long, strong, and sure his fingers were. "A vet clinic across town."

Nodding, I began making myself some toast and felt Sawyer's eyes on me the entire time.

"Can we talk about what happened on Saturday night?"

"I'd rather not." Pulling the butter from the fridge, I waited for my toast to pop. Being dicked around with my feelings wasn't something I relished—rehashing said dicking even less so.

"Cat, will you look at me? You avoided me all weekend."

Reluctantly, I lifted my eyes to his achingly beautiful face.

"I don't know how to navigate this thing," he told me.

"Me, either."

"Usually, when I want sex, I don't think about it… I just seduce my way into the woman's panties. But I don't want to ruin our partnership with it."

"I understand. Look, if it's easier, I'll find somewhere else to live until I get back on my feet." Although where and with what money, I didn't know.

"I'm not saying I want you to leave, Cat." He ran a hand through his hair, letting out an exasperated sigh. "Christ, if anything, I want you to stay here with me. I guess I just want to know I haven't fucked up our friendship with admitting what I did."

"You haven't."

Peering at me over the rim of his cup, he said, "Are you sure?"

"Absolutely."

Sawyer's stare was intense as he studied my face. "Okay, good. Can I ask one thing from you, though?"

"It depends on what it is."

Draining the rest of his coffee, he placed the cup down gently and folded his arms over his chest. "Don't meet Kailon today."

We were back to that?

"Why not?"

"Because I don't trust the fae."

I cocked my head to the side. "In general, or specifically Kailon Perry?"

"It doesn't matter."

"Sure it does."

His jaw tensed as he worked it. "Can you just listen to me once? Not involving the fae is the smartest thing to do right now."

I finished the last bite of my toast and placed my empty cup and dirty plate into the dishwasher. "What if he's the key to stopping whoever is killing these witches?"

"He's not."

"But what if he is? Are you willing to dismiss a potential witness so quickly because you're blinded by prejudice?"

His hands balled into fists under his crossed arms. "You'll be going in blind. You have no idea what he's capable of."

Holding out my arms to him, I said, "Welcome to my life. When am I ever *not* going in blind to supernatural work?" Dropping my arms, I added, "Besides, you can just tell me the rules, right?"

He arched a brow. "Rules?"

"For the fae. I assumed there are some things I can't do or say."

"Even if we started now, it's not enough time for you to learn everything you need to know. A mouse would have a better chance of survival falling into a basket full of vipers," he muttered with a shake of his head.

"You say the sweetest things," I told him, sarcasm dripping from every syllable.

Ignoring my snide comment, he picked up the keys off the end of the counter. "We can talk about it later. We're going to be late."

My badge was hanging on a hook by the door, the sight of it stalling me out for a moment. Sawyer's was beside it, the twin leather-backed shields touching along the long side. Ignoring the feelings two inanimate objects elicited, I snagged the strap of mine and drew it over my head.

My jacket was next, and I tucked my badge inside after I zipped up the leather.

At the elevator, I jabbed the button repeatedly, watching the digital display above the door slowly ascend. Sawyer appeared beside me, his chocolate and whisky scent tangling in my nostrils once more. When the doors opened, I stepped inside.

"I'm sorry," he mumbled, jerking my attention to him.

"What for?"

He peered at me, his gray eyes clear. "For overreacting to the idea of speaking to Kailon. There's bad blood on my end, and I'll be the first to admit that my emotions dictate my rational thoughts, at least when it comes to you, it seems." A heavy sigh escaped him. "I just don't want you to get hurt."

"I'm not sure how much I could mess up going out to dinner," I admitted, then frowned. After clearing my throat, I added, "And now that we've had that chat I didn't want to have, you can tell me what your problem with Kailon is."

"Tonight, after you get home," he promised, then sighed. "We'll talk then. Just promise me—"

"What?"

"Never mind."

The elevator doors opened, and we stepped out into the parking garage underneath the building. I followed him to his motorcycle which he'd retrieved from outside my building yesterday. He handed me a helmet, and I swung onto the back of his Ducati. He kicked the engine to life, and I wrapped my arms tightly around his waist. His stomach muscles went taut under my hands. As soon as he eased the kickstand up, I buried my helmet-clad face in between his shoulder blades, praying that the ride would be a quick one without any side servings of death and flaming wrecks.

Outside, the morning was clear and crisp. Forlornly, I glanced over at the spot my truck had been safely parked on Saturday night before that gremlin had annihilated it.

"How far away is this place we're going to?"

"It's about twenty minutes away," he replied through the comms system. "So, settle back and enjoy the ride."

"Yeah, right," I muttered.

WHEN HE FINALLY PULLED OFF THE ROAD AND INTO THE LOT OF the vet's practice, I scrambled from the back of the motorcycle, my legs stiff from being locked in one position—which was a death grip on Sawyer's hips.

Walking like a green cowboy who'd been in the saddle for eight hours, I followed my partner into the main office of the practice. On the eggshell white walls were posters of dog and cat breeds, ads for pet food companies, and a noticeboard where people were selling pets, looking for lost pets, or offering a service like dog grooming or cat boarding. The linoleum floor beneath our feet was a faint shade of pale blue probably chosen to hide puppy accidents and the inevitable shedding hair of the waiting animals.

My attention snapped back when Sawyer said, "Amy, thanks

for seeing us."

Amy was a dumpy, fifty-something woman with blonde hair, brown eyes, and pink lipstick on her teeth. In pale pink scrubs with navy blue paw prints all over it, she was the antithesis of my only experience with witches so far—which were creepy-as- fuck hags with a penchant for blood-letting.

She smiled at Sawyer warmly. "No problem. What can I do for you, dear?"

"We're wondering if you'd be willing to talk to us about some symbols we can't identify," he said, pulling out his phone and zooming in on the shots. "All we know is they're magical in some way."

I watched as Amy got a good look at the image on the screen. The color drained from her face, her eyes widening with each image Sawyer scrolled through.

She clutched at the neck of her pink scrubs, her round face white. "Were these found at the scene of a murder by any chance?"

I stepped closer. "Why would you say that?"

She stared at me for a beat before returning her gaze to the phone screen. "They're symbols related to death magic."

I rocked back on my heels, dragged back to when Alistair had muttered two words in abject fear—*death magic.* "What else can you tell us?"

Amy glanced around the empty reception area, then back at us. "Let's talk in the break room." Stepping out from behind the high counter of the receptionist's desk, I was pleased to see she was even shorter than me. She led us into a room off the small hallway where more eggshell white coated the walls, the linoleum in this room a mustard yellow instead of blue. Against one wall was a small table set with four chairs. On the other wall was a microwave on a chipped Formica counter, a kettle, sink, coffee maker, and a dish drainer filled with clean cups.

"Please." The witch gestured to the seats. I took one, but Sawyer remained standing. Amy took a seat opposite me, her brow furrowed as she looked at the phone's screen again. "This one here?" She pointed to a symbol that looked like a squat picnic table. "This means altar. And this one?" She flicked to another photo of a symbol that consisted of one long vertical line, a circle at the bottom and a 'c' shape on the top. "This one means death. Alone, they don't mean anything, but when found together…" She shook her head and placed the phone onto the table between us. "Did you find any raven feathers or perhaps a dead raven at the scene?"

"Both."

"Oh, dear. That's… that's not… that's not good," she muttered. She seemed to be talking to herself. "Was the victim also a witch?"

"Would you expect them to be?" I asked when Sawyer remained silent.

Amy's gentle eyes were guileless. "Well, yes. A witch wouldn't waste this power on a human. They must want something from the victim… something intangible that they couldn't physically take. This witch is—" She stopped. Frowned. Rubbed her forehead. "No, but that doesn't make sense," she muttered to herself. "Why would they…"

I glanced briefly at Sawyer, whose face was unreadable. "Why would they do *what*?" I prodded Amy when she stalled out on her rambling.

Amy blinked her brown doe-like eyes at me like she'd forgotten I was there. "Create a death curse. Any experienced witch would know that forcefully taking the ability of another makes the power… twist and warp."

"Warp?"

"Well, yes, dear. Magic is all about balance. If it's taken by force, it resists."

"And these symbols," I tapped on the screen. "They help with the death curse?"

"They *are* the death curse. These symbols combined strip the victim of their abilities by *collecting* them. There's only one problem with that. With the transfer, the magic is watered down upon the death of the original host witch."

Sitting forward in my seat, I rested my elbows on the table and clasped my hands together in front of me. "Do you know of any witches in the area who might be able to do this or *want* to do this?"

Amy shook her head. "The kind of people capable of doing this…" she gestured to the phone, "… don't run in the same circles I do. My family has always practiced natural magic."

"Is that where you learned, your family?"

"My mother," she replied. "All power is passed onto children through their mother."

"And what power was passed to you from your mother?"

"I can locate people… locate things."

"Like a Seeker?"

Her face scrunched up in distaste. "No, dear. Seekers require bodily fluid to determine the location of a person. My kind of magic… *natural magic*… only requires a memory or a photograph. I'm what's called an Echo."

I looked over at Sawyer, who nodded and said, "Thanks, Amy. We appreciate your time."

I stood, shutting down Sawyer's phone and handing it to him. "Yes, thanks, Amy. Can we come back to you if we find out anything else?"

"Of course, dears," she replied absently, looking off into the middle distance. "Of course. Anything I can do to help…"

WHEN WE ARRIVED BACK AT THE STATION, I COLLAPSED INTO the chair behind my desk, jiggling my mouse to wake up my computer. I needed a good hit of caffeine to try and get my brain back into gear. Speaking to Amy had chewed up a good couple of hours of the morning. Everything the witch had said made my mind whir. Death curses? Another witch forcibly removing powers? Warped magic? I didn't like magic to start with, but the idea that magic could *warp* made the hairs on the back of my neck stand on end.

"Busy morning?" Brax asked, interrupting my introspection. A fellow member of PIG, Brax was a werewolf from the local

Helheim pack.

"Kind of." I clicked into my emails, checking to see if there was anything important. There wasn't. "Did you hear about the witch fight?"

"The one that brought down your building? Yeah, I did. Are you all right?"

"I'm still alive," I replied with a shrug.

Brax grinned. "Can't keep a good woman down. Any leads on the case?"

"Some. We spoke to one of Sawyer's contacts this morning. She gave us some information that was useful."

Brax nodded. "That's good. I'd better get back to it. Wolfe wants these reports on his desk ASAP and since no one else in this department is at their desks for more than ten minutes a day…" He continued to grumble about his secretarial role, and I let him.

Spinning around in my chair, I dragged my keyboard closer, then clicked into the database that contained information of every supernatural being who had been arrested or questioned in relation to a crime. Since PIG was just a baby organization, the database wasn't big, but maybe I'd find something in there about the red-haired witch I'd seen in Sharyn's apartment. After scouring the reports from Thursday night until today, I found a whole lot of nothing, with the exception of the unfortunate incident at my apartment building and the remodeling of my car by Gremlins "R" Us.

When Sawyer returned ten minutes later, he was carrying a

couple of cups of coffee. He handed me one, then sat. Perching myself on the edge of his desk, I watched as he opened up the 'human' log of arrests and responses to incidents. "What are you looking for?"

"The incident report for the death of Kailon's niece. What day did he say she was murdered?"

"Thursday night."

Sawyer scrolled through every single entry for that date and came up with a whole lot of nothing. The only incidents listed for that night were a couple of break-and-enters and a suspicious fire set in an old tire factory.

"I've already checked the PIG database, and there's nothing there either." Sliding off the edge of the desk, I flopped into my chair and started spinning myself around slowly. "How in the hell are we supposed to investigate a crime that didn't happen?" I asked, thinking out loud. My desk phone rang, and I picked it up. "Yeah?"

"McKenzie, call on line one."

There was a *click*, then I hit the button with the flashing light beside it. "McKenzie," I answered.

"Cat McKenzie, how nice it is to hear your voice again," Kailon purred into the receiver.

"Kailon?" I turned to look at Sawyer, whose eyes flashed with jealous anger.

"I was calling about tonight."

"Tonight?" Sawyer shook his head and mouthed the word *lunch*. I gave him a funny look. He *wanted* me to go now? "Can we make it lunch instead? Today?"

He chuckled, the sound of his voice like barbed wire against my skin. There was something seductive about it, but I knew that one wrong move would cut me to ribbons. "Eager."

"I need to speak to you about your niece."

"I see you're prepared to see things my way, then," he mused.

Whatever. If that's what he wanted to believe, he was welcome to.

"So, lunch?"

"Meet me at Silk at twelve."

Silk? That was the restaurant across town, the one that required men to wear suit jackets and women to wear pearls. "I won't be able to get in there dressed as I am, and if you think I'm going to get changed for you—"

"I own it. Twelve, sharp." And with that last declaration echoing in my ear, he hung up. I placed the receiver down with a shaky hand.

"What time are you meeting him?"

"Midday at Silk." After one revolution in my chair, I stopped it facing him. "You want me to go speak to him now?"

He nodded, then turned his gray eyes back to the computer. "Yes."

"Why the change of heart?"

Gesturing to his screen, he said, "It's clear we need to question him about his niece's murder since there's nothing in the system about it. Plus… you were right. I was letting my own issues cloud my judgment."

A grin flashed onto my face. "Did the great Sawyer Taylor just admit that I was *right* about something?" I turned to Brax. "Hey, Brax, did you hear that? Sawyer said I was right!"

He flashed me a thumbs up, then got back to work again. I glanced around the empty office, wishing the other members of PIG were there so I had more witnesses.

"Are you quite done?" Sawyer drawled, amusement inflecting his voice.

"Not even close," I replied, unable to wipe the smile from my face.

He redirected his eyes back to his screen. "Can we get back to the case?"

"Sure," I said with a shrug. "But talking about how I was right is *so* much more fun." When he didn't take the bait, I sighed. "What are you looking for?"

"Any other crimes that have occurred in the last month that don't make sense."

"Don't make sense as in?"

"The evidence doesn't add up, or there's something about it that isn't logical."

"You think magic covered up some of the scene?"

"Perhaps," he murmured, his fingers flying deftly over the keyboard.

"But that's a pretty slim chance of getting a hit on a crime that could've *possibly* been committed by our suspect and covered by magic."

"Maybe but think about the scene. What would you note as

something that the responding officer might miss?"

I thought about it for a minute. Aside from the destruction caused in my apartment building, the things that really stood out were the use of magic when those symbols were carved—which as far as I knew, no humans could feel or recognize—and the…

"The feathers. Raven feathers were spread out around the body."

Sawyer tapped some more words into the search, then said, "Look at this." He gestured to the screen. It was a report on a woman who was found dead in her apartment. The official cause of death was acute myocardial infarction, AKA a heart attack. "Look here, it says there was a single raven feather found under the body when it was moved."

Scanning the report, I stopped when I got to the person who'd reported finding the body. It was the woman's daughter.

Jesse Fitzpatrick.

Sawyer checked the time, then logged out. "Let's go and see what we can find out before you have to meet that fae for lunch."

7

Sawyer pulled his motorcycle up to a small house in a quiet dead-end street and cut the engine. Pulling the helmet from my head, I dismounted, scanning the street. I found nothing but mid-priced cars parked in driveways, winter-ready gardens, and picture-perfect houses. Nothing about this suburb screamed *'there's a witch living here'* but I'd learned that witches were adept at blending in.

Jesse Fitzpatrick's Victorian home was set back from the road, the still green lawn bifurcated by an aged red brick pathway. A set of five shallow brick steps led the way onto a small, covered porch that was straddled by two huge topiaries in the shape of what looked like budding roses.

In the garden beds along the front, heavily blooming lavender and fuchsia shrub roses grew in orderly rounds, the branches not daring to spill out over the pathway that led around to a side gate.

Sawyer knocked on the door while I admired the flowers that shouldn't be in bloom this close to winter. Reaching out, I touched one fat blossom, the contact making my opal flare with heat.

The door suddenly opened, and I scrambled up the steps behind Sawyer. "Jesse Fitzpatrick?"

The slender twenty-something woman using the front door as a shield nodded. The movement sent one strand of silky black hair over her shoulder. "Yes? Can I help you?"

"I'm Detective Sawyer Taylor." Pulling out his badge from the inside of his jacket, he showed her his credentials. Gesturing to me, he added, "This is Officer McKenzie. Do you have a moment to talk?"

She nodded, tucking her long hair behind her ear and stepping away from the huge oak door. "Sure."

Jesse led us into a living room painted soft lavender, complimenting the warm honey color of the hardwood parquet floor and the large area rug in the center. Around the rug was a loveseat in a darker shade of lavender and two armchairs upholstered in cream. Three of the walls were framed by botanical prints of roses and lavender. Below them were narrow tables filled with indoor plants—verdant and lush. On the fourth wall, three bay windows looked out onto the front garden and flooded the room with natural light.

Jesse sat on the lavender loveseat and folded her arms over

her chest protectively. "What do you want to talk to me about?"

"About the death of your mother, Sara Fitzpatrick." Sawyer settled into one of the armchairs opposite her.

"If you're here to make fun of me again…" Jesse began in a small voice, her jaw tight and her eyes downcast like she was afraid she was being rude.

"We're not," Sawyer told her. "We're with PIG. Do you know what that is?"

"The paranormal unit?" She eyed Sawyer first, then shifted her gaze to me.

"I'm the human liaison," I blurted out.

She nodded. "What do you want to know?"

"Do you mind if I record our conversation?"

The woman pulled her legs up underneath her, reminding me of how a young child being left in the company of strangers might act. "That's fine."

Sawyer pulled out his phone and tapped at the screen. Leaning forward, he placed the device down on the table between them. "Can you tell us what happened on the night of the second of November?"

She swallowed roughly. "I went over to my mother's house to help her with… something, and when I walked in, I found her body."

"What were you helping her with?" Sawyer asked.

When Jesse hesitated, I said, "We know what you are. If your mother was a witch, then you are, too. It follows on the maternal side, right?"

Maybe I was going in blind with that assumption, but my opal didn't lie.

She stared at me for a full minute. And when she finally spoke, it was in a hoarse whisper. "How did you know?"

"Just a hunch. So what were you helping your mother with?"

"We're white witches," Jesse said suddenly. "We don't hurt anyone."

"I never said you did, but I appreciate that you told us," I replied.

"Jesse, can you tell us more about what happened the night you found your mother?"

She squeezed her hands together until her knuckles were white. "I went over to help her with a blessing spell. When I got there, her door was unlocked. She never left her door unlocked." She sucked in a breath, met Sawyer's eyes first, then mine. "She was lying in the middle of the kitchen, cut open from her throat to her belly button. Symbols had been carved all over her torso."

"Where were the feathers?"

If she was surprised by my line of questions, she didn't let on. "They were arranged around her body, the quills directed at her."

"White witches are traditionally weaker, correct?"

Sawyer's question made her bare her teeth. "We're just as strong as any black witch. We have natural magic rather than stealing the life source from others like a black witch does. My mother was the matriarch of our coven. She was the strongest of us all."

"You said you have natural magic. What was your mother's?"

"She was a pyro. She could manipulate fire… create flames in her hands."

Fire.

The witch who killed Sharyn had hurled fireballs at me. Could Sara have been the first victim killed by our red-haired witch? I looked at Sawyer and knew he'd pieced it all together too. With a subtle nod, he confirmed my theory.

"Was there anything else at the scene that struck you as odd?" Sawyer asked. "Maybe something the cops who investigated didn't see although you could?"

Jesse swallowed and clasped her hands more tightly together. "They couldn't see the markings, the feathers or the fact that she'd been… disemboweled. Their official cause of death was a heart attack. I tried to tell them what I saw, but they laughed and fobbed me off. Nobody would believe me."

"Why in the hell were regular cops sent to this?" I asked Sawyer quietly.

"If the responding officer didn't think it was magical in nature, they wouldn't have called PIG. Clearly, some sort of cloaking spell had been used on Sara, shielding the truth from human eyes."

"That's messed up… just saying."

He nodded and returned his attention to Jesse. "Did your mother speak to you about anything strange happening or people she'd recently met?"

"Nothing, no. My mother suffered from agoraphobia. All

coven meetings were held at her house, and I regularly delivered provisions for whatever spell she was working on. She was much loved in the coven."

"Who's leading the coven now?" I asked.

"My Aunt Penelope, although be it reluctantly."

Well, there went my theory of a power play. "What's your power, Jesse?"

The witch looked around the room at the plants and flowers then back at me. "I can manipulate the growth and production of flowers and fruiting trees. Granted, there's not much use for my particular power anymore, but a hundred years ago, my kind of magic was most important, especially in rural areas where farming not only brought money in, but often fed more than one family in the town or village."

"And your Aunt Penelope?" Sawyer asked, sitting forward and reaching for his phone.

"She's a Vreme… she can control climate and weather."

"Were there any windows broken or doors unlocked when you found your mother?" I walked over to the middle of the bay windows and checked the mechanism.

"Not that I could see."

"So maybe your mother knew this person and let them in?"

Jesse frowned. "I don't know. She was incredibly security conscious. I can't imagine she'd just let anyone she didn't know into her house."

Sawyer ended the recording and stood, pocketing his phone. "Thank you, Jesse. You've been a great help."

Walking to the door, Jesse murmured, "Do you think you might know who killed her?"

Sawyer's evasive reply was, "We'll let you know as soon as we do."

When I made it back to Sawyer's motorcycle, I put on my helmet, then waited for him to get on before sliding on behind him. He kick-started the engine, the purr of the expensive engine humming through me.

"What did you think?" he asked, his voice sounding like silk through the speaker in the helmet.

"I think we need to figure out who this red-headed witch is, and soon."

"Whoever she is, she uses death curses to steal the powers of other witches. So far, we've confirmed that she's stolen from two witches… first, Sara Fitzpatrick and secondly, from Sharyn Wyatt. Their powers were pyro and seeker, respectively. She's stolen a third power, though… we just have no idea what it is."

"You mean Kailon's niece's power?"

"Right. You need to find out what that was over lunch today, Cat. I'll drop you off at the restaurant on the way back to the station."

8

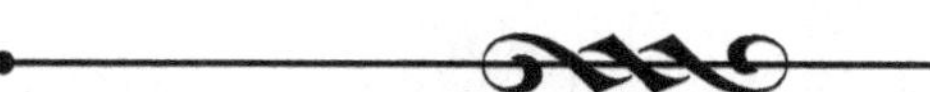

I walked into the restaurant's vestibule right at midday and immediately felt like I didn't belong. Everything about this place screamed expensive, from the gold-leaf ceiling to the carpet that was so thick underfoot I could've curled up and taken a nap. The host looked at me from behind her solid gold podium, her eyes running down my body disapprovingly.

"Can I help you?" She asked the question in the tone of *You are dog shit on my shoe, peasant.*

"Ah, Kail—"

"She's my guest, Amanda. Thank you," a man said, coming toward me dressed in a black pinstripe suit. The suit was paired with a black silk shirt and tie. "I'm so glad you came, Cat McKenzie."

I frowned. I didn't recognize him, but he sure as shit knew

who I was. He tried to lead me deeper into the restaurant, but I resisted. "Who are you?"

The man's face seemed to melt away, revealing angular cheekbones and glowing green eyes. "Kailon?" I hissed, looking around to see if anyone else had noticed the miraculous transformation.

He smiled. "The one and only. Come now, Cat. You're making a scene."

"You think I give a shit about embarrassing you?" I shot back.

He chuckled, resuming the face of another man. "I really don't."

"Where'd you get the face? Did you kill someone for it?"

"No… no death necessary. I've just manipulated my appearance a little so I'm not recognized."

"Yeah, exposing the world to the things that go bump in the night is a real celebrity booster."

Laughing softly, he led me to a table in the back, somewhere private where we could talk. I took in the restaurant as he pulled out the seat opposite me. If I thought the front vestibule was glamorous, it had nothing on this. I had to squint with how much gold was on the ceilings, the crystal chandeliers winking and reflecting more and more of the lustrous light. More gold was on the balustrades that led patrons up and down the shallow steps. The restaurant was built on different levels, with the table Kailon had led us to being at the very back and on the very highest level.

"We'll have our privacy here," Kailon said.

"Said the spider to the fly."

The fae's eyes danced with laughter, but before I could open my mouth, a server appeared and snapped out the heavy linen napkin from beside my elbow, placing it in my lap. Jesus, I felt like I was a child who couldn't be trusted to keep the food in its mouth.

"I'm glad you came, Cat," he drawled.

"I came because you have information we need."

"It bothers you that you need me, doesn't it?"

"It bothers *you* that you need *us* just as much."

That shut the bastard up.

I grinned at him. "Don't be a dick today, Kailon. You need us more than we need you."

He smirked, flashing his teeth. "Let's discuss the arrangement I posed to you on Friday."

"The one where we catch the witch so you can kill her painfully and without mercy?" I asked incredulously.

The air in the room seemed to still, then grow cold as he said, "Yes."

"We can discuss that later. Firstly, we need to know what you know about your niece's murder. We couldn't find the report for her death."

"She was murdered in Wonderland. That's why you couldn't find anything on it."

"For fuck's sake," I said, throwing my hands up and pushing back from the table. "We don't have any fucking jurisdiction in Wonderland. What do you want us to do?"

I tried really hard to keep my voice down, but judging from the stares of the few diners in the restaurant, I was failing. Kailon waved his hands around lazily, causing my ears to pop.

"Did you do the bubble?" I asked, glancing around trying to see the damn thing. "That crazy-ass bubble that blocks things like you did in the witch's apartment?"

He looked smug. "I could murder you in your seat and nobody would see it."

I narrowed my eyes at the fae, annoyed. "Cleanup would be a bitch, though," I told him. "How would you explain the body?"

He shrugged, the fabric of his suit shifting like it was a second skin.

"Tell me about Moira's murder. I need to know everything."

He sighed, and his bravado slid off him until all I could see was a man… er, male who was still grieving. "I found her at her home. She'd been laid out like that other woman had been, her stomach opened up, symbols carved on her body."

"And she was a witch?" I had to be sure that the threads we'd already pulled together could take another strand. At his nod, I asked, "Can the fae also be witches?"

"Yes."

"Tell me what her power was."

He took a sip from the glass of water on the table, then placed the tumbler back down carefully. "She could manipulate the will of supernatural creatures."

"Fuck," I muttered, staring at him. *The gremlin.* Sawyer had said their brains were so small that they wouldn't think to terrorize the city all on their own, but if it had been sent here, that was a different story. Clearly, the red-headed witch had also stolen Moira's powers, but to what end? What was she trying to achieve?

Kailon's human guise melted away from view, replaced with those slitted reptilian eyes. "You know something, Cat McKenzie. Tell me what it is," he demanded, the 's' and 'z's of his words exaggerated and drawn out.

"That's not the deal we have," I said carefully.

He bared his sharp teeth, and I caught a flash of fangs. "We don't have any deal."

"Then I'm definitely not telling you," I shot back, thankful my breath stayed steady. It was never a good idea to show the monsters you were scared.

"Fine," he eventually said, everything about his appearance returning back to normal. With an irritated wave of his hand, Kailon broke the barrier that hid us from plain sight, and my ears popped. The soft chatter of the other diners and the clink of cutlery on fine porcelain plates filled the tense air between us, going stereo in my ears.

"Are you ready to order, sir?" a server asked Kailon, popping up out of nowhere.

Kailon rattled off a couple of dishes, then handed him back the menu.

"I hope you don't mind that I ordered for you," he said after the server had gone, his civility back in place, although I could tell he was tense.

"Would it have mattered if I did?" I replied. I hated men who assumed things I'd like to eat about as much as I found short jokes funny. Taking a sip of my water, I let out a deep breath and asked, "What's going to happen to the witch when we catch her?"

There was no inflection in his voice when he said, "I'm going to slowly torture her to death."

I raised my brows at him. "You do realize you just admitted premeditated murder to a police officer?"

The smirk didn't drop from his lips. "You yourself said you had no jurisdiction in Wonderland, so that's a moot point. Whether I commit murder or not, if it's done in Wonderland, you can't do shit."

Dammit. I hated it when the bad guy was right. "Why did you do it?" I asked.

"What?"

"Why did you take on that job for Marcus Davis? The one who made you have an epic mantrum and reveal the existence of the supernaturals to the world?"

His pale brows rose, his eyes dancing with amusement. "*Mantrum?*"

"A man-tantrum. They're worse than any three-year-olds."

He actually laughed at that. "I like that, Cat. *Mantrum,*" he repeated, testing out the word. "But in answer to your question, I did it because that little fuck Davis pointed the finger at me in order to save his own skin. He was money-grubbing. He had no honor. Him throwing me under the bus like that only served to confirm that impression."

"Did you have to make it so… graphic? I mean, we saw *everything*."

"Yes. I needed everyone to understand that the fae aren't to be fucked with. We're not the winged, glitter-sprinkling balls of light so often depicted in the movies. The fae are a cruel race who adhere to the old ways."

And I was beginning to understand just how bound to the rules the fae were.

"You said before that there were fae who controlled even you."

"There are."

"Who?"

He paused for a beat, and I looked behind me to find the server approaching with our food. We both sat in strained silence while our meals were carefully laid out onto the table in front of us. Once the guy was gone, Kailon said, "There are two warring powers in Wonderland, the Seelie and the Unseelie courts. Two queens rule, one light and one dark. Astrid is the Seelie queen. She rules with benevolence and grace. Avi is the Unseelie queen. Where her sister is pure, malice corrupts her heart."

"Who's ruling now?"

"Avi, the Unseelie queen. Her dominion is in the seasons of fall and winter."

"And Astrid's are spring and summer?"

"And they each serve six months a year?"

Kailon gestured to the risotto in front of me. "Please. It's delicious."

I didn't want to eat anything, but for the case, I would. Picking up my fork, I scooped up some rice and ate it.

Kailon's brows rose. "Good?"

I swallowed. "It's okay." The fae smiled. "Are you going to answer my question?"

"Time moves differently in Wonderland. Winter isn't December through to February, nor is summer June through August. A queen's rule can last decades, sometimes even centuries."

"What's Avi like?"

He smiled a serpent's smile. "Mad. Murderous. Malicious."

I narrowed my eyes. "She sounds like a peach. Why are you telling me this? It can't be common knowledge."

"It isn't, but I feel like you need to trust me, Cat McKenzie, and the only way I know how to do that is to tell you truths that are generally not known. You know I cannot lie, so you know what I tell you now is truth."

Swallowing a mouthful of water, I considered his statement. Knowing he couldn't lie to me did put me at ease, but that didn't mean he couldn't bend the truth as he knew it. Omission was just as dangerous as admission. "And what do you want from me in return?"

He gave me another one of his cold smiles and sat forward to pick up his knife and fork. He cut into his bloody steak, his eyes on me the whole time. "I want to know all there is to know about you, Cat McKenzie. I want to know where you came from."

I swallowed. Playing this game with him was likely to leave me bleeding out. I didn't want him to know more about me than he already did, but he was right. He shared, so I should share too.

At least I got to choose what to share and how much.

"My mother died when I was ten. My father when I was nineteen. I decided to join the Force after his death. I've lived in Buxton my whole life."

"Anything else?"

"Nothing. I'm just a cop doing my time with PIG."

He cut a piece of steak and popped it into his mouth, chewing slowly. "I think we're a lot alike, you and I."

"How do you figure?"

"We both like to play games with the truth."

9

"**G**irl, you came!" Sasha exclaimed, wrapping her arms around me carefully and squeezing. "I knew you couldn't resist seeing Mike in his MMA shorts for that long," she added with a wink.

I laughed, the grin not falling from my lips because this was my happy place. I loved being in the fighting gym, that sense of belonging still strong even after my two-week absence.

"You got me."

"So what are you doing here? Are you working out?"

I shook my head. "No beating the crap out of things for another five or so months, I'm afraid. I just came to see if you wanted to go to dinner after class tonight. My treat to make up for the shitty-friend status of late."

"Yes! I've missed our regular catch-ups."

"All right, let's get started," Mike called out, ending our conversation.

Sasha groaned, but there was a smile on her face. "The sadist awaits," she told me with a smirk.

"Hashtag blessed."

"I heard that, Sasha," Mike yelled, making us both laugh.

"Go, before he starts making you do box jump burpees as punishment."

Sasha shuddered, blew a kiss to me, then walked onto the mats with everyone else.

"Everyone start warming up," Mike told them. He watched for a moment before barking out, "Pick up your knees, I want to see them at torso height. No slacking… Jesus, Sasha, stop talking."

I smiled and sat back, insanely jealous as I watched the class I couldn't be a part of for another torturous one hundred and fifty days—not that I was counting or anything. At least my knee had been healed. It was a small consolation, I guessed.

When the class wrapped up and everyone started to leave the mats, Sasha walked toward me with her bag slung over her shoulder, that gorgeous sweat-sheen of hers all glowy.

"Jesus, why can't you be ugly when you sweat like everyone else?" I griped.

She grinned, dabbing at her brow with a towel. "Jealous bitch."

I shrugged. It was true enough. "Are you ready to go?"

"Yeah, let's do it. I'm starving."

We waved goodbye to Mike on the way out, hitting the pavement and strolling toward the pizza place a few blocks away.

It was one of those old-fashioned restaurants where you could grab just one oversized slice of whatever you wanted, and it would only cost you a couple of bucks.

"How have you been?" she asked. "You know with everything that's happened to you since the vampire thing?" I'd made sure to keep Sasha up to date with everything happening in my life. Her wrath was simply not worth it.

"Ah, where to start." I opened the door to the pizza place and stepped inside. "We're working a new case right now. My apartment got condemned when two witches had a slugging match with magic. I moved in with Sawyer. A gnome healed my knee under my partner's request. And my new truck got crushed by a gremlin."

"Oh," she said casually. "Is that all?"

Yeah, Sasha could handle my crazy shit. "You want the usual?"

She nodded. "I'll grab a table."

I wandered up to the counter and smiled at the guy standing behind it. "Dante, how's things?"

Dante was a first-generation Italian who ate, breathed, and slept his restaurant. "How are you, Cat? You and Sash want the usual?"

"Please. And can we grab a couple of beers to go with it?" I asked, putting on my *pretty please* face.

Dante grumbled something about being too soft on them and ducked into the back to grab some beers from his personal stash. He wasn't supposed to serve alcohol—he wasn't licensed to—but it wasn't like I was going to rat him out. I'd lose my favorite pizza place.

He returned with our drinks and slices, and I dutifully carried them on a tray over to Sasha, who was sitting at our regular table.

"Twist Dante's arm again?" she asked, taking a sip of her beer.

"I have to use this badge for something good, right?"

She laughed.

"So, are you still seeing Dylan?"

"Dylan?" She looked confused. "Oh! Dylan, the plumber, is gone."

"Why?"

"He had a weird little toe on his left foot. Seriously, it looked like a peanut… a shriveled, flesh-colored peanut."

"Oh, yeah," I replied dryly. "You gotta kick those guys to the curb."

Sasha stuck her tongue out at me. "Dylan was replaced by Shane."

"Shane the…?" We'd devised a system not too long ago to give each guy a title based on either his profession and/or a descriptive adjective for the size of his dick. That way, Sasha (read: me) could keep all the men in her life straight.

A dreamy sigh. "Chef."

"Got it. What's he like?"

She shrugged. "Doesn't matter because he was replaced by Brad, the personal trainer, a couple of days ago."

"What was wrong with Shane?"

"He didn't go down on me enough."

I coughed, spraying beer everywhere. "I have no words, Sash."

She barked a laugh. "Ha! That'll be a first."

She took a bite of her Hawaiian pizza. "Brad's amazing, though. He's so fucking good in bed, too. You know, he's one of those men who makes sure his partner is satisfied multiple times before getting his own O."

"How big is his dick?" I knew Sasha. She measured them all and plotted them on a chart.

"A solid eight," she replied.

"Lucky girl," I murmured.

"So, what about you? I hardly know what's going on in your life anymore. Are you dating? Have you met someone?"

Snagging one of the paper napkins from the holder in the center of the table, I wiped my fingers, then crushed it in my hand. "Unless you count the fae assassin I had lunch with today… no."

"Did you know he was fae? Did you know he was an *assassin?* Oh, girl, please don't tell me you let him between your legs."

I threw the greasy napkin at her. "I didn't. And eww… I only met him because he's supposed to be helping with our case."

"All right. What about you and Sawyer?"

"What about me and Sawyer," I asked warily.

She dropped her slice onto the paper plate and stared at me. "Cat, please, you've been silently drooling over your partner for weeks now."

"You know, drooling by definition is a silent action," I pointed out. "And it's not been weeks. It's been two weeks. *Weeks* like you said it implies, like, five. At least three."

"Semantics."

I dropped my half-eaten slice of pizza onto my paper plate and drained my beer. "Nothing can happen. There's too much at stake."

She rolled her eyes. "I'm not talking about getting married to the guy here. I just think you should screw him and get it out of your system. At least then, you'll know exactly what it's like and you'll be able to move on and focus on finding an emotionally available man."

"What? That's a terrible idea."

"But with everything else that's happening in your life, I think you should cut your losses and get an orgasm out of it."

"What if it damages everything, though?"

She heaved a heavy sigh like we'd talked about this ad nauseam before. "Have you actually discussed this with him?"

"Kind of? He admitted he had feelings for me, but we both agreed it would ruin our relationship if we gave in to the impulse. Plus, given his nature, he couldn't remain faithful. It's physically impossible."

Sasha plucked her own napkin from the holder and dabbed at her mouth. "Okay, so this is me looking at it from a purely analytical point of view. You both want to fuck each other's brains out. The fact that you almost did at that club kinda proves that."

I wanted to point out that we were under the influence of a spell at that time, but she waved away my questioning look.

"You also don't want to break the dynamic you have at work, and I totally get that. You already know he'll be sleeping with other people after you guys have your one night together, so what you need to do is convince yourself that it's just a fuck. No emotions means you can both get what you need, right?"

"I feel like you skirted right around the ruination of our working relationship," I muttered.

"And I feel like you're using it as an excuse. You're a woman who knows what she wants, and what you want is Sawyer's dick, so why don't you go and get it?"

"This has to be the worst advice I've ever heard," I muttered, poking my finger into the cooling cheese on my slice. "So you're saying I should sleep with him, ignore my emotions, and get on with life?"

She wiped her hands on the napkin. "Yeah. Pretty much that. If things get strained, that's on you. He was honest about what he could give you. You can either choose to accept that or not, but if I were you, I'd be all over it. The guy is to-die-for smoking hot."

"Your advice is the most convoluted shit I've ever heard."

"Stop thinking and start feeling," she added, punctuating each word with a jab of her finger into my arm. Tilting her head to the side, she looked at the watch on my wrist. "Shit, is that the time? Brad said he was coming around tonight." She stood, slinging her sports bag over her shoulder.

"Wouldn't want to keep lover boy waiting then," I said with a smirk. "Go get that dick."

She held up her hand for a high-five. "You, too."

I finished off my slice of pizza, then waved goodbye to Dante as I left.

"Be careful out there, Cat," he called.

"Will do."

Stepping from the restaurant, I huddled into my jacket and began the three-block walk back to Sawyer's apartment. I glanced around, frowning at the dim lighting. Normally, the lights of the city buildings were almost offensively bright in the darkness, but tonight they seemed dull in comparison. The new moon hovering above in the inky sky didn't do much to improve the visibility of the ice-slick sidewalks either.

The wind came up then, pushing at my back. Whipping around me in a violent gust, it filled my ears with howling whistles and white noise. Burrowing deeper into my jacket, I peered up into the night sky only to have my eyeballs sandblasted by the icy wind. Squinting to ease the sting, I focused on my feet and trying not to fall on my ass as I hustled back to the apartment as fast as I could. Something didn't feel right here.

My head jerked up when the streetlight above me exploded, raining sparks down onto the sidewalk and into my hair. I flinched as, one by one, the other streetlights surrounding me died the same death, the bulbs exploding in a shower of sand-fine glass and a whisp of smoke. When the last of the lights blinked out, I was surrounded by suffocating darkness. My opal flared white-hot in warning around my neck, and I clutched it over my jacket, spinning around, squinting into the shadows that seemed to be growing thicker by the second.

The sound of glass ground under a shoe made me spin around...

... just in time to see a fist coming out of the darkness and flying at my face.

"Shit." Twisting to one side, I avoided the brunt of the hit, taking the punch on the left shoulder instead. Rubbing at the joint, I spun around, retreating to the relative safety of the exterior wall of a nearby building. Blinking, my night vision came in slowly, the shadows and voids turning into discernable shapes before morphing to lank red hair and bared white teeth.

When I got a good look at the muddy-brown eyes of the witch we were chasing, I said, "It's you."

"Yes." She smiled malevolently. Between one breath and the next, a ball of spitting blue flames manifested between her palms. With the flick of a wrist, she sent the fireball careening in my direction. I dove out of the way, the flaming ball slamming into the wall and extinguishing with a hiss.

Determination flashed in her eyes, another fireball forming in her hands. Volley after volley, she sent my way. And I dodged them all until I was doubled-over and wheezing through my open mouth.

With the flick of her wrist, she readied another ball of flames.

"Timeout," I pleaded, flattening my palm and making a 'T' with my free hand. "Timeout."

She snuffed out the flames, a triumphant smile on her face. "All I want is the necklace. Give it to me, and I'll spare your life."

I shook my head. "Sorry. No can do. I barely do what *my partner* tells me, so you have no hope."

A cruel smile formed on her lips. "You can't beat me, you know," she purred. "My power grows with every witch I kill, and I will continue to kill until I've had my revenge."

"You really like the sound of your own voice, don't you?"

She growled. Oh, yeah, that was a growl of frustration—I'd recognize it anywhere. "Give it to me."

"Nope. Not going to happen. You're under arrest. You have the right to remain s—" I yelped as a blue fireball came toward me where it crashed into the wall beside my head, the sound of bricks cracking filling my ears.

"Give. It. To. Me."

My eyes darted around the too-quiet street, and I let out a relieved breath when I saw Reaver propped up against the fender of a parked car. "No. Don't make me add resisting arrest to your rap sheet. Now, stop being a pain in my ass and let me arrest you."

Jesus, I sounded just like Sawyer.

I skirted closer to the parked car. "Why have you been killing witches?"

"You've found the others then, have you?" She laughed. "I thought it would've taken you a lot longer."

"You're making quite a mess."

"Amassing power is a messy job. Now, give me the necklace."

"No. You've been a very bad witch. No necklace for you."

Lunging for Reaver, I felt the hilt immediately warm under my palm and brought it between us, daring her to attack.

She hissed, her eyes narrowing first on Reaver, then my chest where the opal sat beneath my shirt and jacket. Drawing herself up, she cupped her hands and attacked. The fireball she launched closed in fast. I used Reaver to parry the flames like I was playing baseball, returning each and every fireball she sent my way with a satisfying *thunk*. Reaver hummed in my hands as flames licked the steel like a lover, and I grinned at the witch through the dissipating flames and smoke.

She screamed at me, her face twisting with rage.

"Use. Your. Words!" Another step. I needed to get within range so I could pistol-whip—or rather *sword*-whip the witch. I needed to knock her the fuck out, so I could arrest the woman, take her to the station, and stop all this madness.

With another scream, she drove into me, sending us to the cold pavement with a grunt. The fall knocked Reaver from my grasp, and it slid across the ground—spinning—and came to rest a few feet away near a building.

Her lip curled off her teeth in a fierce smile when she saw I'd been disarmed. Moving like quicksilver, she straddled my waist, pinning my arms at my side with her thighs while wiping blood from the bridge of her nose. With a smear of crimson across her nose and brow, she slashed at the zipper of my jacket with long, claw-like nails, sending snow-white, downy feathers into a tailspin around my face.

"Hey, this is my favorite jacket," I griped.

Ignoring me, she slid her hand into the top of my sweater, her sharp fingernails scraping across my collarbones. She loomed above me, her long red hair dragging against my face and neck, getting stuck in my mouth.

"You should try eHarmony if you're looking for a date," I said, spitting out the lank strands as I tried to wriggle from her grasp. "I hear their success rate is phenomenal."

As she got closer to the stone, I sensed a vibration in the opal thrumming through my skin.

Through my muscles.

Through my blood and bones.

Why wasn't it blasting her away like it had done before with the fireballs?

I wasn't going to wait around to find out. My arms may have been pinned, but my legs weren't. Drawing them up, I slammed my knees into the witch's lower back, throwing her off balance. She toppled over my head, her hand sliding out from inside of my sweater. Before she could recover from the fall, I leaped to my feet, bouncing on my toes like Mike had taught me to do in class.

I glanced over at Reaver, the witch following my gaze. For a beat, we stared at each other, waiting.

I dove for the blade.

She dove at me, knocking me off balance. The collision sent me hurtling in the opposite direction to my salvation. My head slammed into the corner of the building, pain exploding through my temple. Blood—wet and hot—gushed from the wound.

Vision flickering, I tried to remain conscious, reaching my arm out for Reaver.

Then…

… then it was dark.

When I woke, I had no idea how much time had passed. Reaching up my arm, I touched the gash on my head, wincing. Bringing my fingers down, I rubbed the sticky blood between my fingertips, staring at it…

My necklace!

Lifting the neck of my sweater, I searched for my necklace, clutching at the empty space it used to occupy. A cold ache settled into my chest, an icy throb that mimicked my breaking heart. It felt as if I'd lost a piece of my soul. I looked around for Reaver, but it was gone too.

Slowly getting to my feet, I began making my way back to the Astoria Building, praying that Sawyer wasn't home when I got there. I didn't need him to see me like this—with a bloody face and down feathers stuck in my hair. It was like I'd lost a fight with a gaggle of geese wearing brass knuckles.

The doorman stared at me as I walked through. He opened his mouth—clearly to ask me if I was okay—but shut it when I glared at him. Once I was inside the elevator, I looked at my reflection in the doors. The gash on my head looked horrendous, blood streaming from the wound, dripping off my chin to the floor.

When the car slowed to a stop and the doors opened, I stepped out, looking around to make sure there were no witnesses. Pulling the keys from my zippered pocket, I opened the apartment door.

Sawyer was in the kitchen, so he got a good look at me before I could escape down the hall and into my room.

"Cat?" he asked, dropping his dishtowel onto the counter. When I said nothing, he demanded angrily, "Cat, what the hell happened to you?"

Ignoring him, I wandered into my bedroom, into my bathroom, and flipped on the light.

Sawyer followed me. "Cat?" His voice was cold and deadly. Dangerous.

I glanced at him as I rifled through the under-sink cupboard, looking for a first-aid kit. "What does it look like? I got my ass handed to me."

"Who did this?"

Placing the kit on the counter, I shucked my shredded jacket and began looking for the saline and gauze, but my hands were shaking so badly I couldn't keep them steady enough. Sawyer took over for me, gently easing me down onto the closed toilet lid.

"Who did this?"

"The witch," I said. "She ambushed me on the way back from dinner with Sasha."

"Jesus."

He crouched in front of me, touching the saline-soaked gauze to my temple. He dabbed at the gash, his eyes serious. They roiled with color, and I could've sworn I saw lightning flash in their depths. I kept my mouth shut and continued to watch his face. He looked ready to commit murder.

"Has Reaver shown up here tonight?"

"No. Was it with you?"

"It was until I got knocked out cold." I looked at him, panic brandishing a gun at my carefully constructed calm. "Do you think she took it?"

"I wouldn't worry about that." Dab. Dab. "The sword is only loyal to you." Swipe. Swipe. "It doesn't look like you need stitches," he murmured.

I fell silent, just breathing in through my mouth and out through my nose, trying to calm the calamity of thoughts. My necklace was gone.

It was *gone*.

The last thing my father ever gave me.

The last physical representation of his love for me.

Gone.

Sawyer stopped suddenly, his arm dropping. "Are you in any pain?" he asked softly, brushing the back of his fingers across my cheek. "You're crying."

I swiped at the wetness, at the evidence of my unraveling, and drew back my shoulders. "I don't think so unless my pride counts?"

He studied me, removing the backing on one Steri-strip and applied it to my head. "Something else is wrong. Tell me."

A sob got stuck in my throat, and I swallowed convulsively. I touched the center of my chest, praying I felt the necklace there. That it had all been a horrible dream. "She stole my necklace,"

I croaked.

"She *what?*"

"She stole the opal."

He pulled back. "Why would she do that?"

I shrugged. "If I knew, I would tell you."

"What's so special about that stone?" he wondered out loud, pressing down the other side of the butterfly strip and dumping the bloody gauze and wrappers into the trash.

My words came out in a jumble. "I don't know. All I know is that my father gave it to me for protection, and I was never supposed to take it off. I wasn't supposed to take it off. And now it's gone. It's gone…"

Sawyer suddenly tugged me closer, holding me against him. Burying my face against his chest, I wrapped my arms around his neck and tried to shove my emotions down, down, down, but the tidal wave of grief and pain was too strong. I felt consumed by them.

"Shh, it's okay, Cat. It's okay." Pulling away, he tilted my chin up so I had to look at him. His eyes seemed to reflect my complete and utter devastation, but that compassion was edged with determination, with flashes of rage. "We'll get it back."

Sawyer picked me up in his arms and left the bathroom, taking me to my bed. With a gentleness I wasn't expecting, he lay me down onto the comforter, then moved to my feet, taking off my shoes. "You need to rest," he said.

I watched him through puffy eyes, still rubbing tears from my cheeks as he removed each shoe. When he reached for the button on my jeans, I let him take them off too. Tucking me into bed in just my sweater and panties, he sat beside me.

"Everything will be better in the morning."

"How?"

Sawyer shook his head and tucked a strand of hair behind my ear. "Trust me?" He stood, leaned down, and brushed a kiss against my forehead. "I'll let you get some sleep."

10

"**P**ussy cat, wake up."

Sawyer's voice was soft and low in my ear. I cracked an eye and looked at him.

"There's been another murder…"

My other eye opened.

"A woman's body was found in Buxton Municipal Park…"

All my senses came back online.

"Discovered by a jogger this morning. Same injuries as the other victims. Get up. Get dressed. We need to leave in ten minutes."

Sawyer left the bedroom, and I threw the quilt from my body, sliding from the bed. Although I still felt the loss of my opal, I also felt a little more in control. The shock was gone, leaving me with a fire burning inside me. I was going to get it back and give that witch a spanking she'd never forget. Dashing into the bathroom, I washed my face, used the facilities, and emerged once more to get dressed.

Five minutes later, I was standing in the kitchen with a cup of coffee in one hand and a slice of toast in the other. I ate quickly, carefully avoiding Sawyer's intense gaze.

"How are you feeling?"

I rubbed at the spot over my heart. "Sore. Hollow, but better than last night."

"I swear we'll get it back for you."

Finally raising my gaze, I looked at his handsome, determined face. "I know." I took a bite of my toast. "I'm sorry about last night…" I paused for a second. "About falling apart like that. Crying like a girl is definitely not my style."

"You don't have to apologize for being vulnerable with me."

Vulnerable. Yeah, that about summed it up. I hated being vulnerable. "I'd rather not talk about it anymore. It doesn't change the fact that it's gone, but you can bet your ass I'll be making sure I get my necklace back. And I'll make that witch rue the day she ever thought to take me on."

"Hell hath no fury," Sawyer murmured, a hint of a smile on his face.

Popping the last of the toast into my mouth and draining what was left in my coffee cup, I put my plate and mug into the sink and dusted off my hands. "Let's go and catch a witch."

Sawyer pulled his Ducati to a stop outside the gates of

Buxton Municipal Park fifteen minutes later and shut off the engine.

Clambering off the back of his bike, I propped the helmet onto the seat and asked, "When will PIG get unmarked cars?"

A smile whispered across his face. "Not enjoying being on the back of my bike?"

"I'd rather have my truck back."

"Wolfe is trying to get funding for us, but because we're—"

"I know, I know," I interrupted. "Because we're so small and niche, we're unlikely to get anything out of the department." There was police tape on the gate posts, the yellow tape like catnip to curious humans who took a morbid interest in crime scenes. There were at least a couple of dozen there now, most of them dressed in their active wear even though they weren't currently being very *active*.

Looking past the gates, I saw that the elm and northern red oaks that grew alongside the winding path were bare having lost their battle against winter, the evidence littered at their bases.

I smiled when I saw Smith wander up the path and duck under the yellow line. Putting him in his place always made me feel better. "I knew this was for the freaks," he muttered under his breath, flashing me a look filled with rage and hate.

Lucky for him, I had fantastic hearing. "You know you love to see me, Smith."

He sneered, his top lip curling off his teeth and his eyes darting to something behind me.

"We got a problem?" Sawyer asked in a cold, hard snarl, his

hand coming to rest on the small of my back.

Smith's eyes narrowed on Sawyer and for a moment, I thought we'd have a fight on our hands. My money was on Sawyer. Smith needed an ass-whooping.

"Do we, Smith?" My partner's voice was a warped growl so low I wouldn't have been surprised if only dogs could hear it.

"No," Smith muttered before turning and walking away. Aww, I was looking forward to that guy busting my chops.

Peering over my shoulder at Sawyer, I asked, "What did you do?"

He looked at me—all innocence and goodwill. "What do you mean?"

"You know what I mean. Why was Smith so nice to me just then? And by nice, I mean why did he not start supe shaming me like he did last time?"

He shrugged. "Maybe he's had a change of heart."

I rolled my eyes at him. "I'd find it more likely that he was threatened with changing his heart than any moves made off his own back."

We strode through the park, and I took note of the charred trunks of trees as we passed, and when I looked over at Sawyer, he had a frown on his face.

"Lots of fireballs got thrown around last night," he murmured.

I nodded.

We made it to a white rotunda that was wrapped with more police tape, a half dozen Buxton PD milling around—all not wanting to get too close. I got that. Nobody wanted to mess with a paranormal crime scene, especially not when you could end up cursed, bitten by a supernatural creature, or hunted.

Sawyer held up the tape for me while I ducked under it, my gaze zeroing in on the scene in front of me. An African American woman was sprawled in the middle of the white wooden floor, her curly, black hair fanned around her head. There were scorch marks on her jeans and jacket, and holes and tears in the fabric where she'd been struck by the fireballs.

The front of her North Face jacket was open, revealing a disemboweled torso that had been carved up with the same symbols as the other victims. Around her were small gray and white flecked feathers, the quills pointed in toward her body.

"Well, that's different." I pointed to the feathers then followed a trail of blood that disappeared off the rotunda's white planks. Peering over the edge of the railing, I saw a dead pigeon, its belly cleaved open and its head cocked off to one side in an unnatural angle.

I took my phone out and snapped a couple of photos of it, then looked at Sawyer, who had crouched beside the body.

"Who do you think she is?" I asked.

"I'm not sure." While he got a closer look, I checked out more of the scene. There were more scorch marks and chunks of burned wood littering the floor of the rotunda. The railings had taken a lot of damage, holes punched out every few feet. Catching a glimpse of something contrasting against the white wood, I found her purse. It was dangling from the edge, the strap caught against a popped nail.

"Sawyer," I called. He came over, and I caught a whiff of his chocolate and whisky scent, trying to ignore how good he smelled. "Look."

Reaching into his pocket, he pulled out a set of gloves and handed them to me. Sliding them onto my hands, I picked up the purse and opened it. Tissues. Pepper spray. A Harlequin romance novel. When I found her wallet, I pulled out her ID.

"Samantha Giles," I said. "Thirty-one. Lives not too far from here."

Sawyer checked out the address, then stared in the direction of her house like he could see it through the trees. "Our witch must've caught her cutting through the park to get home."

I nodded with his assessment. "Do you think she was killed before or after our witch attacked me last night?"

"I'm not sure."

I stared into her face, a face that looked calmly serene considering what she'd been through. Did she put up a fight, and if she did, what was her magic of choice?

Magic of choice.

"I wonder…"

"What?"

I turned to Sawyer. "Last night, before the witch attacked me, the streetlights all exploded." Looking down at Samantha. "What if Samantha manipulated electricity and that's what our witch stole?"

"A possibility. Or maybe it was just light she controlled."

"I guess we'll never find out, will we?" I said, sadly. "What time do you think she was killed?"

"Judging by the condition of her body, I'd say between twelve and fifteen hours ago. The ME will give us a more accurate time of death once the autopsy has been done."

He took another look at the ID, then at the purse still clutched tightly in my hands. "Anything else in there that might give us a clue?"

"Look, the girl liked smutty romance books, so she could've been into anything." Still, I dug a little deeper and pulled out a metal name tag that had the logo of one of the luxury hotels in Buxton on it. I flashed him the badge. "She worked at The Palatial."

"We'll go speak to the staff after the ME and CSI are done here."

I glanced up over the railing then to see some of the CSI team arriving. We still didn't have a team just for supernatural crimes, which was stupid, but I wasn't in the habit of making my thoughts known.

Sawyer and I stood back while they worked, instructing the scene photographer to capture all the scorch marks and the position of the feathers. With every minute that passed, I was getting more and more caffeine-deprived. By the time they were done, it was close to ten o'clock.

"Argh, I need coffee," I announced to Sawyer as we walked back to his motorcycle.

"We can get some after we notify Sam's family of her death, then we're heading to The Palatial to see what we can find out."

11

The Palatial was one of the premier luxury hotels in Buxton. It was a fusion of art deco architecture and modern design—a place where the rich and famous of Buxton could come to play when they were taking a break from their glamorous lives.

When Sawyer and I arrived, a doorman opened the huge glass and bronze door, welcoming us inside. After delivering the bad news to Sam's mother, I felt terrible. Losing a daughter was difficult under the best circumstances. Add a death curse into the mix, and Ms. Giles was understandably upset.

I could still hear her desperate words to me as we left. *"You catch this witch and make her pay for her crimes. My Samantha was a kind soul... she didn't deserve this."*

Each clutching our cups of coffee, Sawyer and I headed

straight to the reception desk where a pretty twenty-something was just finishing up a phone call. I watched, annoyed, as she gave my partner the once-over and put down the phone.

"Hello and welcome to The Palatial. Are you checking in?" she asked him, flipping her blonde hair over her shoulder and pouting her filler-swollen lips. She was unashamedly ogling Sawyer—unashamedly flirting with him too.

Bitch.

Sawyer pulled out his badge and flashed it at her. "Detective Sawyer with PIG. This is my partner, Officer McKenzie. We were wondering if the night manager is still here. We'd like to have a word."

Her eyes widened a little, her hand fluttering and coming to rest on her chest in concern. *Girl, please.* All she was interested in doing was drawing attention to her boobs. "Ms. Perkins is out back. I'll just get her for you."

She picked up the phone, hit a number, and spoke quietly into the receiver before hanging up. "You can take a seat on the couches over there." She pointed to a set of plush burgundy and velvet, then hit Sawyer with a mega-watt smile. "By the way, my name's Greta, and I'd be happy to help you with anything else you need…" She hesitated, like she was deliberating on whether she should add *like a blow job?*

With a tight smile, Sawyer said, "Thanks," then walked across the foyer.

I slumped down into one of the couches, balancing my takeout coffee cup on my knee, while Sawyer took the other. I stared at him, wondering whether he was going to go and fuck Big, Blonde, and Buxom behind the receptionist's desk.

"Are you going to feed from her?" I asked, blurting out the words I didn't want to voice.

His brows rose. "From whom?"

I jerked my chin in Greta's directions. "*Whom?*" I mimicked. "The blonde behind the desk."

Sawyer glanced over quickly, his gaze not lingering on her for more than a moment. Greta, on the other hand, had been watching him openly, and when he'd looked over, she began to flip her hair in an almost manic fervor. It was as if she thought there was a direct correlation between the number of times she touched her hair and the likelihood of Sawyer getting into her pants. "She's attracted to me," he replied.

No shit. "Yeah, but are you attracted to her? If she offered to get on her knees right here and now and suck your cock, would you let her?"

His eyes simmered with heat. "I never pass up an opportunity to feed."

Not the answer I'd wanted to hear.

Argh, why was I so jealous?

I got busy looking at my coffee cup.

"Hello," a woman said. I glanced up. "I'm Sally Perkins, The Palatial's night manager. Greta said you needed to speak to me?"

Sawyer stood up smoothly, while I clambered out of my seat like a baby hippo stuck in mud. "Ms. Perkins, thank you for seeing us. My partner and I are here investigating a case, and we were wondering if you could answer some of our questions."

The woman clasped her hands in front of her. "Of course. Let's go back to my office where we can have some privacy."

We followed her out of the glitzy marble and copper reception area and through a door into a white hallway. There were other doors shooting off it on either side, and she led us into one of those rooms, closing the door behind her.

"Please. Take a seat."

I got a good look at Ms. Perkins as she settled behind a flimsy-looking desk covered in files, pens, and Post-it notes. She was an older woman, maybe in her mid-fifties with salt-and-pepper hair and a kind face. She looked like a grandmother, just waiting to impart some words of wisdom. Her dark brown eyes remained on me for a lot longer than was necessary, her gaze flickering to my chest, then back to my face. She gave me a smile when she saw me watching her.

I frowned.

Somehow, that smile looked familiar.

Settling her hands in front of her on the desk, she said, "You said you had some questions for me?"

Sawyer set up his phone to record and placed the device on the edge of the desk. "Yes, we believe you may be able to help us with an investigation involving Samantha Giles."

"Is she one of your employees?" I asked.

"Yes, she is." She looked at Sawyer. "Is Sam in some sort of trouble?"

Ignoring Ms. Perkins's concern for Samantha, he asked, "Can

you tell me if she worked yesterday?"

"Yes. She finished at six-thirty last night, just after I came in."

"Do you know how she got home?"

Her brows furrowed. "She walked. Why?"

Sawyer and I looked at each other. Then, he said, "I'm sorry to be the one to tell you, but her body was found this morning in Buxton Municipal Park."

Sally covered her mouth with her hand, tears spearing her kind brown eyes. "Oh dear, how terrible."

"We apologize for having to do this, but in order to catch who killed her, we're going to need your help." He waited for her to nod, then added, "What can you tell us about Samantha?"

Ms. Perkins eased back into her seat, folding slightly shaking hands in front of her. "She was one of my best reception staff. She was never late. Always went out of her way to ensure guest happiness and expectations. I'm going to miss her." She took a deep breath. "Have you informed her mother yet?"

"Yes, we spoke with her before coming here."

Sally dipped her chin in understanding. "What else would you like to know about Sam?"

"How long had she worked here?" Sawyer asked.

"I hired her about eighteen months ago."

I said, "Did you know she was a witch?"

"Yes, and a quite powerful one at that."

"Do you happen to know her power?" Sawyer asked.

Her eyes flickered to him. "She was a Radiant… a controller of light, and the only Radiant in the country. They are, apparently, a rare breed."

"Why do you know so much about witches?" I asked. "Are you also a witch?"

"No, dear. Sam told me, although she was terrified she'd lose her job." Then she fixed her eyes on me, and I felt the gravity of her stare. Why did I get the sense that she knew me? "She couldn't change being a witch any more than Cat could help being her parents' daughter."

I straightened in my chair, the hair on the back of my neck prickling. "What did you say?"

She gave me a slightly exasperated sigh—just like Mrs. Brown used to give me when I got mouthy—and added softly, "It's nice to see you again, Catherine."

Sawyer was looking between us. "Do you two know each other?"

"No," I said, while Sally said, "Yes."

Another one of those sighs. "Really, Cat, you don't recognize me?"

I squinted at her—you know because that helps you so much, right? The sledgehammer of awareness had yet to hit. Maybe my brain was too busy trying to process everything else that had happened this week—losing my apartment, my new truck, and my necklace all within the space of a couple of days—to work through this problem, but I didn't recognize her. I saw flashes that reminded me of Mrs. Brown, but mannerisms and smiles weren't enough to make one person into someone else.

"Perhaps this would help," Sally said, beginning to shake her head slowly. I blinked as her salt and pepper hair gave way to familiar black curls. Her face changed shape, but her eyes didn't. They stayed kind and dark. I watched, rapt, when she seemed to shrink in her chair, her head and shoulders sinking closer and closer to the top of the desk.

"Mrs. Brown?" I croaked, standing up. I felt rooted to the spot. My heart lurched in my chest.

Could it really be her?

Could she really be sitting in front of me?

"Yes, dear." She stood, and I realized she was just as short as I remembered. Walking around the desk, the top of her head barely met my stomach.

I fell to my knees, tears burning my eyes. I tried like hell to blink them back, but it was a losing battle. I wrapped my arms around her and hugged tightly. She slid her arms around me too.

"Where did you go?" I asked her, pulling away. "I never heard from you after I left for college."

She cupped my face, her palms warm and soft. "You didn't need me anymore, Cat. You'd grown up and were experiencing life."

I shook my head. "But… why did you leave me?" All of my abandonment issues were rearing their heads right now. Fuck.

"Because I had someone else to look after, another young woman who needed my help and guidance."

Guidance? "What are you?" I whispered the question, almost afraid of the answer she'd give me. If she said a banshee or something, I didn't think I could handle it.

"I'm a Brownie, dear. I… help people when they need it for as long as they need it. My ilk is well known for our nurturing nature and fondness for both human and fae children."

"But my parents…" I switched direction and said, "What about Rogue Faction?"

Her eyes widened a little as she brought a hand to her mouth. "You know about—"

"Yes."

"How?"

I got a flash of Draco's face in my mind's eye.

Draco, the vampire who had killed my father in cold blood.

Draco, the vampire who had killed my first partner in order to engineer my reassignment to PIG.

Draco, whose head I took with the help of Reaver.

"A little vampire told me," I replied.

Mrs. Brown nodded slowly, then said, "Your parents knew what I was and kept my secret safe… not that Brownies were ever hunted by Rogue Faction. After your mother's death, your father asked me to look after you. His heart was too clouded by grief and rage to consider your needs, and I was happy to step in." She touched my cheek softly. "After all, you *are* something special."

"Ha!" I said softly to Sawyer. "See?"

He chuckled. "It was never in doubt."

"I have so many questions for you," I told Mrs. Brown. "About Mom and Dad. About who they really were. What they were doing with Rogue Faction."

"And you'll be able to ask them, but now is *not* the time." She patted my shoulder. "You need to find out who killed Samantha because I fear whoever they are, they aren't finished yet."

12

I sat down heavily on my bed, rubbing my face. It had been a long-ass day. After leaving The Palatial, Sawyer and I had returned to the office and tried to come up with a more solid timeline for the killings. What we'd figured out so far was our witch had killed four witches—all powerful in their own rights. She'd stolen their powers, and with that theft, the ability became twisted and warped.

So what did that leave us with?

A serial-killing witch who now had the power to control fire, supernatural creatures, light, *and* had the ability to seek out any living thing. That had been Sharyn's power, but she'd needed an organic sample from the target in order to find them. I wondered if the theft of that power gave our witch the ability to find someone more easily than that.

It was too much to even contemplate thinking about. With a long groan, I let myself fall back onto the mattress. "Oww!" I exclaimed, sitting up again and rubbing the back of my head.

I peeled the quilt away and eyed Reaver lying there. "Huh. I guess you're back."

Picking up the sword, it heated under my touch, and I could've sworn it was happy. Like it missed me. I rubbed my thumb over the etching of my face near the pommel—the same one that triggered it to disappear when needed—and shut my eyes, smiling when I heard laughter echo through the apartment. When I opened my eyes again, the laughter died away, but the warmth remained in the blade. I carried it with me into the bathroom, propping it up on the vanity while I stripped out of my clothes.

Starting up the shower, I waited a few minutes before stepping under the spray. A shower, dinner, then bed. That was all I was planning on doing tonight.

I'd just started wetting down my hair when I heard a metallic *clank*...

Then I promptly screamed as the drain in the middle of the shower floor started to move. I watched as it turned around and around, finally being pushed off by a pair of tiny green frog-like hands.

Reaching over, I quickly turned off the water and avoided looking down. "Nope. Not doing this today," I muttered to myself. Just as I opened the shower door, I screamed. Glanced down. A green hand was on my ankle. I followed the hand to an arm then finally to the body and head of something that looked like the love child of Alien and a kraken… only really, really small.

The green creature's slimy skin glittered with an iridescent shine as it crawled up from the drain. Using its tentacled legs, it stood, reaching its maximum height of little more than three inches.

I must not tell short jokes, I told myself sternly.

The thing looked up at me, blinking its third eyelid over its muddy green eyes. Its forehead was huge, leaving its eyes on the side of its head rather than at the front.

"What are you?" I asked, frozen in place. "And would you mind…" I motioned to its hand on my ankle.

It uncurled its fingers with agonizing slowness, finally releasing me. Nodding in thanks, I stood there for a moment, contemplating my next move. Screaming and running from the room was always a firm favorite, but then I figured there had to be a reason for this creature coming to visit me. I mean, I knew I attracted these things like I was catnip for supes, but come on…

"I am Grindylow," the creature said, its voice muffled like it was speaking underwater.

Grindylow? He used it like it was his name rather than what he was. "And *what* are you doing here?"

He blinked at me with those creepy three-lidded eyes again. "I've come to warn you. My mistress sent me."

"Your mistress?"

He nodded, his tentacle-like hair rocking forward with the movement. The tips curled and writhed like they were alive and capable of independent movement.

"Okay. Sure. Your mistress. What did she say?"

That's right, Cat! Humor the tiny creature and get the hell out of dodge.

"She says she is in danger and needs your help."

Blowing out a breath, I reined in the need to scream. Why was it that supes were always coming to me for help? I didn't want to make friends that badly. Was it too much to ask to be left alone?

"Help with what?"

"There is a witch hunting her kin. My mistress has seen it happen. She fears she is next."

"Well, if I were her, I'd get the fuck out of town."

Grindylow shook his head. "She cannot. She must stay. It has been forbidden."

"Forbidden? By who? Whom? Whatever!" Gah, I hated these supes with their cryptic way of speaking. Although… "Are you a type of fae?" I blurted.

Grindylow nodded slowly, smiling a little. Well, I could've done without that image in my head. Although his mouth was small, it was filled with hundreds of razor-sharp little teeth.

Like a mini-*Jaws*.

"I am one of the oldest fae in existence."

"Yet, you serve a mistress?"

He shot me a look that made the water in my body quake. "Be of care, Cat McKenzie. I may serve another, but that is because she controls me with her power. I am still very old, and I can make your life hell."

"Well, no need to do that," I said dryly. "I'm already living in it, thanks."

He hissed at me. "You need to take heed of my warning. More is coming. Death. Destruction. Deceit."

"I can't wait. They're three of my favorite 'D' words, and when they're used all in the same sentence, you can bet I'm getting excited."

Grindylow's eyes narrowed on me. "Are you always this way?"

"What way?" I shot back. I was getting defensive, but that was because I was scared and maybe a little embarrassed that I was having a conversation with a miniature ancient Alien-kraken-like creature that crawled up out of the shower drain.

Plus, I was naked.

Sooo naked.

"This mouthy."

I smiled. "Aww. You say the sweetest things."

I turned toward the door when Sawyer knocked and called out, "Cat, are you okay?"

"Fine." Returning my attention to Grindylow, I said quickly, "Who is your mistress?"

Sawyer barked, "Cat! Who are you talking to?" He started jiggling the door handle, trying to break the lock.

Grindylow narrowed his eyes on the door. "Rose Sanchez," he hissed then escaped back down the drain, his tentacles slithering after him.

"Cat? Answer me!" Sawyer called out in a growl, slamming his fist into the door.

"No one." Jesus, I felt ridiculous yelling through a bathroom door. Marching over to it, I yanked the door open and stumbled back a step when Sawyer's dark eyes dropped to my naked body.

Reaching out blindly for a towel, I wrapped it around my body. "I just had a visitor."

His brows rose, but there was tension that bracketed his mouth. "I didn't see anyone come in."

"Well, I guess you wouldn't since the bastard came up through the drain. Try to keep up, Sawyer."

He gave me one of his impatient looks, and I smiled. "So why don't you tell me what was said and by whom."

"All right, so I was minding my own business, having a shower when some fae called Grindylow popped up out of the drain and told me his mistress sent him with a warning."

Sawyer blinked. "A *Grindylow* came to see you?"

"He just called himself Grindylow, but yeah. Why? And don't tell me they're some kind of bad-ass fae that I should steer clear of because that ship has fucking sailed."

"Grindylows are notorious for drowning people, especially children."

"Wow, another filicidal supe. Just what I always wanted."

Either Sawyer was getting used to my amazing dry humor, or he was ignoring me because I got no reaction out of him. "The thing is, Grindylows don't serve anyone but themselves and their queen."

"So maybe his mistress is the queen?" I hedged.

"Maybe," he muttered. "I've not heard a whisper about Grindylows in a long time. Not since before I became a cop and moved to America."

"Where were you before coming here?"

"Wales."

Noted.

"Anyway, Grindylows? Do you think this message has come from the queen?"

"I doubt it. The last queen died over a decade ago, and another one hasn't been born to replace it. Their hierarchy is a lot like those of bees. There's one queen and thousands of workers, which would explain why he called himself Grindylow. There's no individuality among them. They have a hive-mind mentality. The queen gives birth to one other female who takes over after her death, but the previous queen never did achieve that. As far as I know, the Grindylow is now a dying species."

"He gave me the name Rose Sanchez. Said it was his mis—"

His phone started to ring, and my eyes darted to his pants pocket. I watched him as he answered the call, his replies curt and efficient. When he hung up, he said, "There's been another body found."

A QUARTER OF AN HOUR LATER, WE WALKED INTO THE 21ST STREET subway station and made our way down the stairs. The place was crawling with Buxton PD, but they were all hanging back like they were afraid to go much further than the ticketing booths.

I glanced around, seeing if there was a friendly face anywhere. All I found was a roomful of scorn and derisive looks. In other words, it was a Tuesday.

"Jesus, you'd think they could send someone competent to come down here." Smith's retort echoed around the underground space, and I turned in the direction his voice had come from. The bastard stepped forward from his group of buddies, his cruel eyes shifting down my body.

"Aww, Smith, you really shouldn't be so hard on yourself." I blew him a kiss.

"Fuck you, McKenzie," he roared, silencing any conversation that hadn't thinned out at our arrival.

"Is that all you got, Smith?" I laughed. "No wonder you're still a fucking beat cop."

He lunged for me, and I readied myself, feeling Reaver shimmer into existence, warm against my palm. Smith skidded to a stop, his eyes sliding down to the blade as he clearly second-guessed his plan to attack me.

"Look," I reasoned. "I don't know what your fucking problem is with me—"

"My *problem*?" he hissed. A couple of the other cops moved closer, one even putting his arm over Smith's shoulder and getting a grip on his chest. "My fucking problem is that you'd rather swan around with the fucking supes than work with your own kind."

"My own *kind*? Oh, you mean you and the other bunch of dicks in the department who wanted nothing to do with me after my partner was killed. Is that who you're talking about?"

Sawyer placed his hand on my shoulder—whether it was warning or support, I didn't know.

Smith glared at me, and I saw everything that was running through his head. His hate. His fear. His jealousy. "You're a fucking traitor," he muttered, shrugging out of the hold of his colleagues. "A monster playing with monsters." He walked up the stairs and out of the subway.

"Come on, pussy cat," Sawyer said softly.

Descending the stairs into the subway and ducking under the tape strung across the bottom, I let my gaze roam over the scene. I couldn't see anything out of the ordinary—it just looked like the subway to me.

"The body was found during a routine inspection of the tracks this morning," someone said behind me. I turned. It was a detective from the department. I didn't know his name, but he looked familiar. "Nobody has touched it since then."

It. Like *it* was an object rather than a human being.

"What else do you know?"

"Nothing. I was just here babysitting the stiff until PIG got here." He shuffled off with a shrug, ducking under the police tape at the base of the stairs and making his way above ground.

"Come on." Sawyer motioned for me toward the tracks. He climbed down the maintenance ladder, and I followed him, wobbling on the track ballasts as he led the way to the victim about halfway down the length of the platform.

I studied the rocks beneath my feet, cursing the way they seesawed and shifted under my weight. How in the hell did our witch get down here with a body, or was our victim lured here somehow? Given how busy the subway system was, the murder had to have occurred sometime between midnight and six o'clock when the trains stopped running. Otherwise, the body would've been discovered earlier than this morning.

"Cat, you'll want to take a look at this," Sawyer called, and I hustled to catch up with him. Crouching down at his side, I took in the scene.

"Same injuries as the other victims."

Sliding on some gloves, he got a little closer to the body. The woman was dressed in an expensive white suede coat and coral pantsuit, her hair and makeup untouched. Her jacket had been torn open along with her white blouse, the same markings as the other women carved into her body.

Sliding his finger up under the edge of her jacket, Sawyer lifted the fabric a little more, revealing symbols that looked as if they'd been carved more deeply.

"She's changing her MO," I said, putting my face closer to the wounds. Yup, definitely deeper. Gesturing to one particularly gruesome mark, I said, "See how extensive this one is? On Sharyn's body, they were almost superficial wounds, but here they've gone down deeper. There's certainly more blood." I glanced around. "No raven this time either."

"Maybe she needs more blood for the spell to work?"

"Or maybe we have a copycat on our hands." God, I hoped I was wrong. I stood up and started looking around for a purse.

Spotting something hidden in the shadows of the platform, I clambered over the rocks, being careful not to disturb too much of the scene.

"Heads up," Sawyer said, throwing me a spare set of nitrile gloves.

Sliding them on, I picked up the coral leather satchel and popped open the clasp. Inside, I found her wallet, a packet of mints, a can of pepper spray, and a Sig Sauer P938 Scorpion.

I showed the gun to Sawyer. "Clearly, she didn't get a chance to use this."

Her wallet was nothing more than a cardholder—her black AMEX sitting in pride of place. Pulling out her ID, I read her name.

"Rose Sanchez..." I paused. *Sanchez*. "She's the woman Grindylow told me about." I looked down at the body. "I guess we're too late."

He nodded and stood, gesturing for the ID. "This is odd. It says she was born over seventy years ago." He peered at Rose's face, then back at the piece of plastic in his hand. "She doesn't look a day over thirty."

He handed the ID back to me. I slid it into the wallet and closed the billfold. When I glanced up, I saw him staring into the mouth of the tunnel seventy yards away.

The hairs on the back of my neck stood on end. "What is it? Sawyer?"

"I don't know. Something's coming."

"Something like a train?" I asked in a whisper. "Because that's not cool." The services were supposed to terminate at the stations on either side of the 21st Street.

"I don't know," he repeated, but I sensed the tension in his body.

I stepped a little closer—looked a little harder—but all I could see was the black maw that regularly swallowed trains and commuters.

Then I felt it…

… a faint wind whispered out of the darkness, gently tousling my hair. Beneath my feet, a weak vibration grew along with the strength of the wind. My hair started to lash at my cheeks, the hum hammered more violently through my body.

I inhaled deeply and frowned. In the air was the scent of brine—brine and the unmistakable odor of stagnant water.

"Sawyer?" I gripped his arm.

"Run." He turned me around and shoved me in the back toward the maintenance steps. "Run!"

I clambered up the rungs as fast as I could. When I reached the top, I offered Sawyer my hand and hauled him up too. Behind him, the track ballasts as well as the tracks themselves began to visibly vibrate, the railroad spikes working their way out of the base plate. The low-level hum grew in frequency until it became an all-out roar. For half a second, I wondered what else the supernatural world was going to throw at me.

Bracing myself, I peered into the darkness to find out what was going to come out of the shadows. A troll? Some kind of uber-fae I'd never heard of before? The Balrog? No, couldn't be one of them. They were *fictional.*

Yeah, just like you thought gremlins were, my brain helpfully reminded me.

Sawyer grabbed the back of my shirt and yanked. "Run!"

My feet got moving even though my curiosity demanded to know what was coming. I glanced over my shoulder to see a solid wall of water spewing out of the mouth of the tunnel, the sound of all that water intensifying until I thought my ears were going to bleed.

"Rose's body!" I yelled over the ear-splitting noise.

"She's already dead!" Sawyer gasped in reply. "And if we don't move, we will be too."

Like a dam release, a violent deluge of water came toward us. Sawyer placed his hand on the base of my spine, urging me forward—toward the stairs that would lead us to the concourse and the ticketing booths. I took them two at a time, until I reached the top where I slammed into the concertina gate they used when the subway shut down in the wee hours of the morning.

It was locked.

I rattled the damn thing, tugging at it, praying it would budge.

Sawyer shoved me out of the way. "God… *dammit!*"

The water was rapidly climbing the stairs now, the spray sitting heavily in the air, soaking my face, hair, and clothes. "What is it?"

"It's chained. Padlocked. I can't break either." I followed his gaze to the steel links wrapped between the diamond-shaped crosspieces of the gate.

"Why not? You're a supe. You're strong."

"I just can't!" he snarled, and I blinked at him.

Did he look gaunt?

I shook my head.

We were locked in here.

Someone had *locked us in*.

My mind raced. The combination of roaring water, soaking clothes, impending death, and irrational anger at being locked down in the subway to drown coalesced in one word. "Fuck!"

"Maybe I can break it," he muttered. "We have to try something."

I turned around and stared at the water. Maybe it would be okay. Maybe once the water reached us, it would just flow through the gate—unless there was so much water it would drown us first before continuing its journey up and out of the...

What the *hell* was that?

"Sawyer?" I asked, trying to keep my voice calm.

"What is it?" he snapped, still trying to break through the chain and padlock. The gate shuddered with each slam of his body against it, although he seemed to be growing weaker by the second.

I blinked some water from my eyes. "You need to see this."

"See what?"

"Just look."

He turned, and his arms fell limply at his side.

"Do you see it, too?" I asked in a whisper.

The wall of water that was creeping up the stairs—that's right, literally *creeping*—had a face. It was our witch, her watery hair curling and falling in front of her piggish eyes. The liquified witch opened her mouth, the roar coming out of it loud enough to make me throw my hands over my ears. Then the water surged, coming at us like a fucking freight train.

Sawyer grabbed my hand a second before the water hit.

My whole body sang with pain, the force knocking some much-needed air from my lungs. I forced my eyes to stay open under the water as I looked at where Sawyer had his hand wrapped around the gate, keeping us in one place. He stared at me with desperate eyes, a desperation I never wanted to see again. If Sawyer was panicking, we were fucked, and I needed him to be confident we'd get out of here.

The water swirled around us like a stationary tempest, a flood only meant for us. Sawyer pulled me up with him, our faces finally breaking the surface.

"The water has hit a barrier of some kind. It's not flowing through the gate," Sawyer gasped. "Once she figures out there's an air pocket up here, she'll shut it down."

I nodded. Kicking wildly, I tried to stay up, to keep my face in the air pocket, but something was dragging me down. I kicked again, trying to dislodge what was on my leg, and I looked down through the water to find Grindylow clinging to my ankle.

It pointed frantically at something on the step at the far end of the stairs. Bobbing up for another breath, I said to Sawyer, "Reaver is here."

He nodded, and I disappeared back into the black water. Debris clung to my body as I pushed against the tide. Grindylow grabbed my hand, trying to pull me down, and I was stunned by how strong he was. Then I remembered what Sawyer had said—that these little fuckers liked to drown children. I sure hoped that wasn't what was happening right now.

Pushing through the water felt like pushing through cement. Every movement was slow—every attempt to push forward like breathing through sludge. Grindylow kept pulling me, though, dragging me closer and closer until finally, I reached Reaver. The sword hummed its approval at my touch, and I lifted it. Grindylow nodded at me and darted away, swimming so fast it was just a blur.

Kicking my legs frantically, I broke the surface of the water. There was less than an inch of space, so I sucked in a gulp of air and ducked back under. Sawyer was back to struggling with the lock, but he backed away when I returned. I shoved Reaver through the gate and touched a link. There was a fizz and a pop of light, and what was left was a hole in the chain, the two sides falling away.

Sawyer gestured to the lock, and we switched places. When I touched the blade to the padlock, I got the same light show. After taking another gulp of air, I touched Reaver to the chain until enough links had melted away for Sawyer to shove the gate back.

Desperate to escape, we swam out like the water would follow us, but it fell to the ground in a wet heap on the other side. It was completely dry on the concourse level. I glanced back at the wall of water, frowning when our witch's face appeared again. Her giant mouth opened in one final roar before disappearing, taking the flood with her. Water rushed down the stairs as it receded back into the tunnel.

"Are you okay?" Sawyer breathed, touching my face as if he was looking for injuries.

I coughed. "I think so? Fuck, that witch is pissed off now." I looked back at the stairs. "How the hell did she do that?"

Sawyer shook his head and clambered to his feet. After helping me up, he stood at the top of the stairs and peered down. "I don't know. However she did it, her powers have suddenly multiplied."

Powers. I touched the spot where my opal used to sit. Having it with us tonight would've given us enough warning to get out, but what if our witch was using it in a different way? What if it amplified her curses?

Out on street level, Sawyer and I emerged from the subway station, dripping wet and shivering. The air was cold on our exposed skin, making me think that hypothermia was well on the way.

Yay! And by the way, insert sarcasm here.

Police tape had been strung up at the entrance of the station, the cops on guard looking equal parts bored and tired. When they saw us though, they straightened.

"What the hell happened to you?" one of them asked. "Why are you wet?"

"Did you know subway stations make *excellent* swimming pools?" I replied.

Both of them gaped as we ducked under the tape and moved toward Sawyer's motorcycle.

"We need to get home," Sawyer said, teeth chattering as he wrapped an arm around my shoulders and pulled me into his body. He weaved a little and although we were just conserving body heat here, I suspected he needed some help staying on his feet. In an odd, synchronized shuffle, we made it to Sawyer's motorcycle.

Reaver was waiting for us already—propped up against the rear tire.

"P-p-please tell m-m-me you still h-h-h-have your k-keys."

While he searched his pockets slowly, I took hold of Reaver and touched the etching of my face, making it disappear. Slowly—like everything in his body hurt—he got on and started the engine. I climbed on behind him.

"Helmet, Cat. You need your helmet," he rasped in a strained voice.

I took what he offered me and slid the helmet onto my head, the sound of my chattering teeth even louder in my ears.

"W-w-what about the b-b-body? We c-c-can't leave her d-d-down there, can w-w-we?"

"I'll c-c-call Ben in to secure the scene."

"Wh-wh-who is Ben?" I'd never heard this name before.

"The W-w-wendigo at PIG."

Wendigo? I tried to sift through my mental supernatural

omnibus. A wendigo was a native American supernatural creature with antlers and a head like a deer, teeth like a wolf, and the body of an emaciated human.

"The *g-g-growling* guy?"

Sawyer nodded.

Well, I wouldn't be sitting on that guy's desk again.

"Aren't th-they cannibals?" I asked. And why the hell did he look human in the office?

Another nod. "I'll call him w-when we get h-h-home."

He rode slowly, returning us safely to the garage parking of his building. When we finally made it upstairs, I'd stopped shivering, but I was still soaked. In my room, I stripped out of my clothes and got into the shower, the warm water helping to take away the ache of the biting cold that seemed to have settled into my veins. I needed to wash my hair. It smelled of stagnant water and had bits of debris stuck in it, but all I wanted to do was fall into bed.

Nearly dying would do that to a girl.

13

I woke up with a start, awareness prickling over me like a lover's caress. I glanced at the clock—three in the morning. I must've been asleep for around five hours. My whole body ached, something I could only blame on the post-adrenaline dump of nearly getting killed in a flood confined to a six-foot radius focused completely on my partner and me.

I too was hot, and when I tried to shove the quilt away, I discovered it was already down near my feet. That was when I realized Sawyer was in bed with me. Trying to shuffle away, he growled and dragged me back into the line of his body, his arm tightening around my middle. He was hard, his erection prodding the seam of my ass. Peering over my shoulder at him, I was stunned by the look of hunger in his eyes.

"How long has it been since you've properly fed?" I whispered into the dark room.

He flexed his hips into my ass, grinding his erection into me with an almost frantic need. "Almost forty hours," he rasped painfully.

"Why haven't you fed before now?" Greta at the hotel had been a sure thing.

He shook his head, his jaw tight and brows locked down tight over his eyes. "It doesn't matter, but I've left it too long… grown too weak. Feeding off lust won't be enough to sate me. I need…" He moaned, arching against me once more. "I need a woman."

Too weak.

Swallowing, I said, "I'll go and find you someone." Although how I was supposed to achieve that, I didn't know. It wasn't like I could just go up to a random woman and ask if she was willing to let an incubus fuck her in order to feed.

"No," he said, lines branching out from the corners of his eyes. Pain. I saw it so plainly on his face. "I need to protect you… to keep you safe from the witch. You can't go out alone."

His concern for me made me melt just a little bit. *Focus, McKenzie.* "Is this what happens when you go too long between feedings?"

His eyes were glassy—unfocused.

Hazy.

Tormented.

"Yes."

Sucking in a shallow breath through my mouth, I asked, "What happens if you don't feed?"

"Unimaginable pain. Weakness… death."

No, no, no. "I'll go and find you someone," I said in a choked whisper.

"It's three in the morning." He pressed his erection into me again, and my eyes shut, lust whipping at my body erotically. "Just knock me out."

My eyes flew open. "Excuse me?"

"In my bathroom, there's a pre-loaded syringe of fentanyl. Get it. It'll knock me out until…"

I sat up, jostling him. "Until when? You die? No!"

He groaned, shutting his eyes tightly as if in pain. "I have a list of females willing to service my needs when I go past the point of civility. They can take the frenzy. I'll call one when I wake up."

Jealousy was a red-hot poker in my gut. My gaze tracked down his body. He was drenched in sweat, his breathing labored. Every single one of his muscles were straining, the veins popping against his skin. At his hips, his erection seemed to reach for me. I licked my lips. I was torn. I didn't want to see him in agony, but if I did this—if I crossed this line with him—I had to be prepared for the consequences.

An erection was a biological response to stimuli. The sex act was simply two people coming together in order to fulfill a primal need. Feelings didn't *have to be* involved. I could totally keep those confusing bastards locked down tight. My hand shook as I reached out and wrapped my palm around his aching cock, the hot hard length kicking in my grip.

His eyes flew open, confused. "Pussy cat." His moan was a plea that made heat flood my body and made me squirm.

"It's okay," I said, my voice shaking. "It's okay, Sawyer. I'm going to make you feel better."

Pumping my fist, I stroked him through the fabric of his sweats, watching his face carefully. His expression hadn't relaxed. If anything, his jaw locked more tightly and more sweat beaded on his brow.

"Am I hurting you?" I asked. "I can stop."

He grabbed my free hand and brought it to his mouth, his tongue darting out to suck on one of my fingers. I gasped, the sensation hitting me between my legs. My core clenched as I thought about his mouth there instead of his fingers, his cock instead of his mouth.

He rolled his hips into my grip. "Don't stop." His usually silver eyes had turned stormy gray.

Nodding, I focused on what I was doing, trying to ignore the pooling heat between my thighs. Lust had me in a chokehold I had no hope of escaping.

"Cat?" Sawyer's hoarse voice had my eyes darting to his face.

"Yes?"

"You're aroused."

"Y-yes."

"Can I… make you feel good, too?"

"Yes," I whispered.

His eyes shut then, like my very answer was euphoric, and

when they opened again, they were a solid black sky flashing with lightning. I realized then that his need to feed was a living, breathing beast within him.

"Lie down beside me."

I did as he asked, keeping my eyes on his face until I couldn't anymore and his fingers brushed against the skin of my stomach. Electricity arced between us, and I arched into his touch, biting back a moan as he rubbed me through the cotton of my shorts.

With a frustrated growl, he shoved my shorts and panties to the side and plunged two fingers into my slick heat. I cried out, an orgasm ripping through me with that first touch. I rode his fingers, barely hanging on to my self-control as he dragged out my pleasure.

He kept his fingers inside me, curling them slightly as he pumped slowly, keeping me riding a knife's edge of pleasure. Reaching out, I touched his chest, skimming my fingers down over the slash of his collarbones, the hard padding of his pecs, and down his shredded stomach.

He had a body made for sin, and I was in the mood for sinning.

Sawyer kissed me then, the meeting of our mouths something love songs should be written about. There was a burning possession in that kiss, and even though I shouldn't have, I opened myself up to it. I let Sawyer in—let him consume me.

Reaching down, I wrapped my hand around his cock, biting my bottom lip when he sucked in a hiss at that first touch, his chocolate and whisky scent intensifying. Pumping my palm up and down, he growled, the sound vibrating along my skin and shooting straight to my core.

Everything about Sawyer was sex. His voice. His smell. His touch. My wanting to fuck him had gone from a genuine desire to ease his pain to a burning need. I *needed* him just like he needed me in this moment.

"I need to have a taste of you, pussy cat."

"Excellent idea," I gasped, releasing my hold so he could do just that. Through slitted eyes, I watched him move slowly down my body, dropping kisses on the bare, hot skin of my midriff.

Anticipation and lust shivered through me, licking at me like Sawyer's tongue would soon be licking at me. Hooking his fingers into the waistband of my sleep shorts, he pulled them down my thighs and off my legs, discarding them onto the floor with a casual flick of his wrist.

A low, pumping growl rumbled from his chest as he stared at me.

Even though the barrier of my panties was in place, he attacked me like I was bare. His tongue swept up the length of the panel, his breath mixing with my already soaked pussy. Hooking a finger into the side, he rubbed his knuckle over my clit, making my eyes shutter and my hands clutch at the sheets on either side of my body.

Sweat beaded on my brow, the intensity of what we were sharing made manifest. I had a brief flicker of thought that maybe this was a mistake, but then Sawyer pulled at my panties until the fabric ripped, then discarded them onto the floor along with my self-doubt.

My legs fell open, inviting him—inciting him to use me however he needed to.

He dove back in without hesitation, sliding his tongue through my folds and drinking me. I clutched at his head this time, lifting my hips to position him where I needed, his warm breath feathering over my skin, nearly sending me over the edge.

When he slid a finger inside me though, that was when I lost it. I came apart around the digit, my inner walls clamping down on him and refusing to let go. Sawyer kept pumping, drawing out my pleasure like he'd made it his personal mission to make me feel amazing.

"Fuck, fuck, *fuck!*" I screamed as the orgasm continued on and on. When that wave had finally crested and my pleasure waned, I found him staring at me with hunger blazing in his eyes. He sucked the fingers that had been buried inside me into his mouth, making little aftershocks wrack my body. He was a bad, bad man, but he made me feel so good.

My gaze tracked down to his tented sweats, carnal hunger swirling around in my stomach.

I had to have a taste of him.

"Stand up," I commanded softly.

He watched me for a moment before sliding off the edge of the bed. His chest was heaving from his rapid breaths, his stomach muscles rippling with the movement. Perching on the edge of the mattress, I reached for the waistband of his sweats, pulled them down over his erection, and let them pool around his feet.

He palmed his cock, running his hand over the head while staring at me intensely. "This should be your hand," he rasped, tugging gently.

"That should be my mouth." I took over for him, running my fingers over his length, stroking him and making his head fall back.

I leaned forward to wrap my lips around the head of his cock. He stepped forward with a groan, pushing himself further into my mouth, then ran his fingers through my hair and held me in place.

"Yes, yes, yes," he muttered as I sucked the head of his cock, swirling my tongue around the crown and hollowing out my cheeks as I took him deeper. He tightened his grip when I got down to the base, his full length nudging the back of my throat. Dragging in air through my nose, I concentrated on letting him feel.

"Jesus *fuck*," he groaned, dragging his cock out before sliding back in again. I kept my eyes on him, watching him watching me. His gaze shifted from my face to my mouth, where he was sliding in and out, in and out. His eyes became molten, his mouth opening slightly as he panted. Pushing all the way in, he held himself there for a few seconds before retreating. Again and again, he pushed himself to the limits.

Running his finger over my bottom lip, he withdrew then bent down to kiss me. His tongue swept into my mouth, the thrust and retreat mimicking what he'd just been doing. "Lay back."

Anticipation hummed through my bones.

I lay down and Sawyer climbed up my body before settling on his side. Lifting his hand, he rubbed his thumb over one of my breasts, teasing my nipple until it was a hard peak. The brush of my tee against it was torturous. Shoving my shirt out of the way, he sucked one nipple into his mouth while he palmed the other in his strong hand.

My legs scissored beneath me, looking for friction because I felt another orgasm coming. Sawyer had a goddamn magic mouth. Reaching between us, he ran his finger over my clit, making me detonate with just one stroke. I bucked against him, rubbing myself against his fingers to prolong the pleasure. I was being greedy, although I suspected Sawyer would be giving me a lot more orgasms before the night was out.

When I finally stopped shaking, he moved off my body, rolling onto his back and taking me with him. My thighs split over his hips, my dripping pussy less than an inch from his cock. I stared down into his handsome face, noticing that the stress that had lined his face was slowly fading.

"I want to see you lose yourself to me," he murmured, running his hands up and down my thighs, sweeping his thumbs closer and closer to my aching core. "I want you to give your pleasure over to me completely. I want you to trust me with it."

"Yes," I whispered.

"I need to have you bare in order to feed. I'm clean, and I can't get you pregnant."

I nodded. I'd been tested when I was in the academy, and I hadn't had time for sex since then. I also knew that the only way to make baby sex demons was for an incubus and succubus to have sex. "Just fuck me already, Sawyer."

He lifted me easily, my pussy hovering over his hips. Reaching down, I dragged the tip of his cock through my folds and over my clit. Jesus, that felt good. I threw my head back and absorbed the sensations, feeling another orgasm building again. He really did have a magic cock. I stroked myself a few more times, and that was all it took. I came apart once more, my inner walls clenching around nothing when I wanted to be filled.

Before my orgasm subsided, I impaled myself on him, moaning out his name when another orgasm chased the first. Sawyer tightened his fingers on my thighs and squeezed his eyes shut, taking it all. When I got to see his eyes once more, they were heavy with lust.

"Ride me, pussy cat. I want you to come at least three more times. I want this to be good for you."

I blinked at him. It already was good for me. I'd never had back-to-back orgasms before. He'd already given me three. "Are you trying to kill me?" I panted.

"No, I'm trying to send you to heaven."

Placing my hands on his shoulders, I started to rock against him, taking all of him inside me. I'd literally slid down on his cock four times when I came again. Flopping down onto his chest, I stared at him through the curtain of my hair. How was this possible? Now I understood why there were some women who just wanted to fuck incubus. If one could give you a dozen orgasms in a night, why wouldn't you chase that high?

Leaning up, I captured his mouth in a kiss that showed him everything I wanted him to do to my body. He was still hard and long inside me, the feeling of fullness urging me to move against him again like a cat in heat.

I lifted myself off him, then sat back down.

Sooo good. It felt *so* good.

Sawyer's hands on my thighs tightened. "Do that again," he rasped.

I lifted myself once more, running the head of his cock through my folds and torturing both of us.

He growled, "Now, Cat."

Lining him up with my entrance, I impaled myself again, the friction causing an orgasm to rip through me, tearing apart any self-control I thought I had.

"That was number six," he grunted, fresh sweat beading on his brow. In two swift movements, he lifted me off his lap and positioned me on my hands and knees. Bowing my head, I looked down the length of my body and watched him rub his knuckle against my soaked pussy. I arched into him, chasing the friction, chasing the release that was just there. His finger disappeared inside me, and I came apart—my gratification drawn out and intense. Moisture ran down the inside of my thigh, and I was horrified that I'd become so wet we needed a tarp to protect the bed.

Sawyer hummed with pleasure as he stroked his finger through all that arousal. "Are you ready for the finale?" he asked.

I nodded, letting out a breathy, "Yes."

He stroked his hand down my back, running his strong fingers over the flesh of my ass. I started to pant at the promise of those fingers. Rocking back into him, I begged him wordlessly to take my pussy and ruin it for every other man. When he positioned the blunt head against me, I could've wept. My over-sensitized flesh welcomed him as he slid inside, each one of my nerve endings firing with each inch he took of me. When he was finally filling me, his hips sat snuggly against my ass. He kissed the base of my spine, taking his sweet time.

I groaned. "Sawyer, fuck me already. All this soft shit is pissing me off."

He gave me a half thrust as he growled, "There's nothing soft about this, pussy cat." I swear my eyes rolled back in my head. "But I'll give you what you want because it's what I want, too."

When Sawyer began thrusting, I lost myself to the rhythm—the rhythm of our bodies moving as one, to the way our breaths joined and mingled, to the way our bodies just seemed to fit with one another. I wasn't a stupid woman who had romantic notions floating around in her head. I knew that once Sawyer blew his load, that this would never happen again—*could* never physically happen again—but that didn't stop me from wanting it to.

Shaking my head, I chastised myself for even thinking about that as an option. I didn't need this again. I just needed to enjoy it right now.

Sawyer's finger dug into my hip, holding me in position as he slammed inside me. When I felt his cock kick, I knew he was close, the truth of that setting off an orgasm for me. The sudden clamping of my inner walls must've caught him by surprise though, because he barked, "Fuck!" He pumped twice more, then roared as he filled me.

I sucked in a gasp that turned into a moan. I felt it all, but I especially felt how his semen had triggered another orgasm. I hadn't been ready for it. I didn't want it. To my already strained body, it felt like torture rather than pleasure, but I rode that bitch like a pro, taking it all in.

My arms and legs collapsed under me, taking Sawyer with me. He rolled off me, laying on his back and breathing heavily. Turning over, I looked at him, committing that relaxed face of his to memory.

Sensing me staring, he rolled his head to look at me. His eyes were black, but even as I watched, his usual cool gray replaced it.

"Are you okay?"

I nodded.

"Thank you." His voice was serious, and I was stunned to see that all the strain and pain that had been on his face was now completely gone. His skin was tanned and healthy again, his movements strong and sure.

Tilting my head back, I looked at the clock on the side table and gaped. "We've been fucking for four hours. Is this what it's like every time?" The instant that question was out of my mouth, I regretted it. Waving my hand in front of me, I added, "No. Don't answer that. I don't want to know."

Capturing my hand, he brought it to his mouth and kissed my fingertips. "I should leave you to get some sleep. But thank you."

My eyes were already shut. "You probably need to go and refuel, I guess. Eat a dozen eggs. Drink some Gatorade," I quipped.

He chuckled softly. "You have an hour before you have to get up. Get a bit more sleep, pussy cat."

14

I t was a little after eight o'clock when I rolled out of bed. I was surprised by how good I felt considering I'd only gotten an extra hour of sleep. After a quick shower, I got dressed and wandered into the kitchen to get some coffee. Sawyer was already there, dressed in black slacks and a black business shirt with the cuffs rolled up to his elbows.

Damn him and his sexy forearms.

The top couple of shirt buttons were undone, giving me a glimpse of the smooth, tanned flesh of his chest—a chest I had touched last night.

"Good morning," he murmured, making me realize I'd been staring.

Averting my eyes, I mumbled, "Morning," and eyed the carafe of fresh coffee on the counter behind him.

He leaned against the smooth black granite and folded his arms. "Are things going to be weird now?"

"God, I hope not," I replied, clambering up onto one of the kitchen stools. I motioned for him to pass me the carafe. He did one better—he poured us each a cup. He even added a couple of spoons of sugar into mine. *Was he going for sainthood?*

I made grabby hands at him, and he passed one over with a smile. Once I had that cup in my hands, I took a sip and let out a content sigh.

Heaven.

Peering at him over the rim, I asked, "Why? Was it weird for you?"

"No. It felt… natural. Right."

I squirmed in my seat. Took another sip of coffee. Cleared my throat. I needed a new subject to get away from the way my stomach fluttered at his admission. "So, you still haven't told me about your beef with Kailon. You promised you would on Monday night."

At the mention of the fae's name, his whole demeanor changed. His shoulders tightened. His jaw set. A growl escaped his lips.

"You promised you would," I reminded him.

"I did no such thing."

"Come on," I whined. "I've had a rough week."

He let out a hard sigh through his nose. "You're infuriating."

"You love me," I said, smirking.

Sawyer shook his head, and I was sure he was going to deny me once more. But then he unfolded his arms and said, "Three years ago, I was working a case that I knew involved a fae. Supernaturals hadn't revealed themselves to humans yet, so I had to do my own investigative work while my human partner chased his tail trying to follow leads that didn't exist. The perpetrator was a boggart… a malevolent spirit, who had been terrorizing a boarding school. Maiming children mostly, but there had been at least one death, too. The boggart escaped into Wonderland once it knew I was getting close, so I followed it."

Dragging fingers through his hair, he created furrows. "I'd investigated crimes in Wonderland before, but I was never overt about it. I'd never gone in uniform like I had that day, so the fae felt as if I'd tricked them somehow. I was detained. I later found out it was under Kailon's orders that I was locked away."

"How long were you stuck there?"

"About two hours, but as you know, time in Wonderland moves much more slowly. When I got out, five days had passed. The boggart had killed six more students in that time, forcing the boarding school to close."

"So you figure Kailon has the death of those children on his hands?"

His nod was stiff. "If the bastard had just left me alone, those six kids would still be alive. Their parents would *still* have their children."

Okay, so now I got it. Kailon was a prick, but really, I kind of already knew that.

My head jerked up when there was a knock on the door. Sawyer was instantly on alert. He motioned for me to stay where I was, then headed for the door, picking up his Glock as he went. From my vantage point at the kitchen counter, I could just see the front door if I craned my neck.

Which I did.

Because I was nosey as fuck.

He pulled open the door, and I felt the tension physically ripple through the room.

"What are you doing here?" Sawyer's voice was a crawling growl.

"I don't have time for this. Let me in," Kailon said in a commanding tone. It was a peek at the deadly fae I knew him to be under the mask of civility he wore so well.

Sawyer stepped away from the door, and the fae was suddenly filling the space with his presence. When he saw me, his eyes quickly tracked down my body, and despite being fully clothed, I felt a faint current of air caressing me like ghostly fingers.

"Cute parlor trick," I quipped, sliding off my stool until my feet touched the floor. "Is that the only way you can touch a woman?" He flashed me a dark smile. "What are you doing here?" I asked.

My gaze flickered to Sawyer, who came to a stop behind Kailon's shoulder. He was glowering at the fae, and after that story, I couldn't blame him for being pissed off.

The fae glanced at Sawyer over his shoulder, then dismissed him by turning to face me. "Baba Yaga was killed last night."

"What?" I demanded, straightening.

"How?" Sawyer hissed at the same time.

"How do you think?" Kailon asked, strolling into the kitchen to pour himself a cup of coffee from the carafe. Sawyer stalked after him, placing himself between Kailon and me. "The witch got to her."

"And *killed* her?" I don't know why I was surprised. I'd accidentally got into a fight with the legendary Baba Yaga when I'd stumbled into Wonderland. She looked like a frail old woman, but man, she made the aquatic stars of Shark Week look like a bunch of pussies with what she was packing in dental hardware.

"Yes."

"And more likely stole her powers too, right?"

Kailon narrowed his eyes at me as he took a sip of coffee. "And that's a power you don't want in the hands of a mass-murdering witch."

I looked at Sawyer briefly—just to see what his reaction was. He still looked pissed. "And what *was* her power? I mean, aside from eating children because yum."

The fae cocked his head to the side. "Necromancy."

I backed up a step until the counter jabbed me in the spine. "Necromancy as in… raising the dead?"

"She fed off children in order to power her spells. There's nothing like virgin blood to raise the dead."

"I shall keep that in mind," I mumbled, clutching my stomach as it roiled with the news. "So we now have a witch running around with the abilities to seek people out, control others, wield fire and water… I'm assuming that was Rose's power since the witch flooded the subway… control light *and* to top all that off, she can now raise the dead? Did I miss anything?"

"No, that was quite the comprehensive list," Kailon drawled.

I glared at him. "Sarcasm is *not* appreciated in times of crisis." Unless it was my sarcasm. I blew out a breath. "Who the hell is this witch?" It was a question more for me than anyone else.

"I've been doing some digging," the fae said, reaching into his pocket for his phone. "I was looking through the photographs the news outlets have been splashing around after each incident, and I noticed something. She was there, at each scene. She was part of the crowd salivating for the ME to bring the body to the ambulance."

Kailon turned his phone in my direction, scrolling through each image with his thumb. He was right. He was goddamn right, and neither Sawyer nor I had even thought to check this. A lot of murderers liked to watch the police discover the body.

I tried to remember who was standing outside the subway station when Sawyer and I emerged. I couldn't remember seeing a crowd, but could the witch have been watching from a distance?

"So who is she?" Sawyer asked gruffly.

"I spoke to a fae in Wonderland who owed me a favor. She recognized the symbols. This witch…" he tapped at the screen, "… is from a very old and very powerful family who can trace their lineage back to the first tsars of Russia. About three decades ago, her family, the Chernov family, were decimated by another powerful coven, the Morozovs, in the western United States. Where and why I don't know. All I know is it was a long-standing feud that was thought to have left no survivors on the

Chernov side. The Morozovs went into hiding afterward for fear of retribution from other covens. Kseniya Chernov, it seemed, did survive, although it's not known how."

"Do you have any idea where she is right now?" I asked.

The fae shook his head. "I'm not a witch. I can't track people like a Seeker. I have no idea where she is, nor do I know where she'll show up next."

To Sawyer, I asked, "Are there any Morozovs in America? Do you think Kseniya will be going after them next?"

"I don't know. We'd have to start going through the databases," Sawyer said.

I returned my attention to Kailon. "Th—" I started, then stopped. I could've kicked my own butt for almost telling the fae thank you. I had to be more careful. "We appreciate what you've found," I ground out.

And from the smirk on Kailon's face, he goddamn knew how close I'd been too.

"Where is Baba Yaga's body now?"

"Still in Wonderland."

"What do you want us to do?"

"What do I want *him* to do is a better question," Kailon said, jerking his chin at Sawyer. "You can't enter Wonderland," he reminded me pointedly.

Sawyer shot me a look. He was warning me to stay quiet about my ability to enter Wonderland when it should have killed me.

"So Sawyer goes and then what?"

"He processes the scene."

"Wait. How in the hell did Kseniya get into Wonderland in the first place? I mean, this is the second time she's gone in, but witches are humans with magic, right? They're not a kind of fae."

Kailon's jaw was tight, and I could tell he was even more pissed off with the witch. "We still don't know, but I suspect her father may have been fae. That part of her blood appears to be strong enough to enter Wonderland."

"And to kill Baba Yaga," I tacked on helpfully.

"Yes." He practically spat the word at me.

Sawyer folded his arms, the movement capturing my attention. I watched the way the muscles in his forearms flexed with the movement, and fuck, I wanted another round with him. His eyes were suddenly on me, the air between us crackling with need. His eyes turned stormy with lust for a brief second before he shook his head and fixed his attention back onto Kailon.

That's right—no lusting after my partner in mixed company.

"Since this death is part of our ongoing investigation, I'll process the scene," Sawyer said. "Cat can wait outside with the EMTs. Once Baba Yaga's body is out of Wonderland, I'll process everything and get our ME to do an autopsy."

Letting out a sigh through my nose, I drained the last of my coffee then said, "Where's the entrance to Wonderland right now?"

"At the docks," Kailon replied.

Still? So much for the entrance moving all the time.

"Okay. Let's do this."

15

When we arrived at the docks, I shivered into my jacket—the hairs on the back of my neck prickling as dread slithered down my spine. I wasn't expecting such a visceral reaction to coming back to this place. Can someone say PTSD? I know I could. My first walk into Wonderland had been no picnic. In my defense, I hadn't even realized I'd wandered in there, and meeting Baba Yaga that time had been *such* a bonus.

For about a week, I'd had nightmares of old ladies with rows and rows of shark teeth in their mouths, smiling at me sweetly. I couldn't stand to look at anyone over the age of sixty—and kind of still couldn't.

Kailon was ahead of us, walking with all the confidence of a fae who feared no one and who everyone feared.

"No matter what, you stay out here, Cat," Sawyer said in a low voice beside me.

I glanced at him quickly. "No problem. You think I actually *want* to go back in there?" I jerked my chin at the lined-up containers that indicated the entry into Wonderland.

"No, but I know sometimes you don't think."

"What's that supposed to mean?" I whisper yelled at him.

"It means you often do something without thinking all the repercussions through. Wonderland isn't a playground. You got in last time, and although I don't know *how*, I think it may have had something to do with your necklace. Now that that's gone, I don't want to think about what could happen to you."

I let the smirk I felt pulling at my lips slide away. "If I didn't know any better, Sawyer, I could've sworn you were concerned for my safety."

He turned his head slightly in my direction, frowning. "Just promise me you'll stay out here."

Giving him a quick salute, I reached for my necklace out of habit, missing the damn thing once more. Although it was a rare black opal, it was more than just a stone. It was comfort and the memory of my father. It was protection and love. It was all I had left of my family, and I wanted the damn thing back.

"You have Reaver with you?" he asked, breaking me from my thoughts.

I touched the now invisible hilt at my side. "Yes. Although, I don't even know why I bother bringing it anywhere. It just shows up and disappears whenever it feels like it." Yes, I was still grumpy about that, but it wasn't like I could reliably count on it. It showed up when it thought I absolutely needed it, and not necessarily in life or death situations.

"Good. Keep it close. And no matter what you hear, don't come into Wonderland."

I rolled my eyes at my partner. "You're worse than a mother with all the fussing you're doing, Sawyer. Has anyone ever told you that before?"

Leaning over, he pressed a chaste kiss to my forehead. "I've never had anyone else to care for, pussy cat. I'm kind of enjoying the role."

With nothing to say after that declaration, I refocused my attention on the sound of Kailon's footfalls.

"We're wasting time," the fae called impatiently right before his footfalls disappeared completely as he stepped inside Wonderland.

I slowed to a stop while Sawyer continued on.

He paused a few feet away. Turned. "Stay safe. Don't do anything stupid," he told me. A ghost of a smile whispered across his mouth, and he disappeared into thin air too.

I let out a breath, seeing it hover in the air in front of me. Snuggling into the department issued PIG jacket, I tucked my hands under my armpits and settled in for the wait.

I'd probably been standing there about ten minutes when I heard a vehicle pull to a stop behind me. Looking over my shoulder, I saw an ambulance and a squad car about fifty feet away, parked side by side. I even let out a groan when I saw who got out of the squad car—Smith. Just what I needed.

He and the EMTs wandered toward me, and I felt my shoulders tighten at their arrival.

Smith's gaze drifted over my face, his mouth twisting in disdain. "You always seem to be here, McKenzie."

"It's my job, you asshole."

"Yeah, you and the freaks get along really well, don't you?" he spat back, hatred coating his words in barbed wire.

Reaver became visible at my side, making Smith's eyes slide down to the blade. I saw a flash of fear in them before he barricaded those emotions up once more.

"Hey, hey, let's just all calm down," one of the EMTs said in an annoyingly placating voice, stepping between us. "We all don't want to be here—"

"McKenzie does. She fucking loves the supes," Smith sneered.

My hands hiked up on my hips. "I don't *love* the supes, shitheel, but they certainly treat me with more professional respect than what you're showing me."

"That's because you're a freak just like them."

My eyes darted to the white spittle gathering in the corners of his mouth. *I wonder if I should tell him. Gross.* "How do you figure?"

I didn't know why I kept taking the bait. No, that's a lie. I knew exactly why. I hated it when people made assumptions about me. They could underestimate me all they wanted—that was actually kind of fun—but putting words in my mouth or automatically assuming something about my character was something I couldn't stand.

"You're not coming back to the department, are you?"

I blinked at him. That wasn't something I'd discussed outside of Wolfe's office. "And what if I'm not. I doubt you'd miss me that much."

He spat at my feet, then rubbed a hand over his mouth. "I wouldn't. I want you gone. What you did to your first partner should have seen you thrown off the force."

"Wow. Not big on forgiveness, are you?"

"Letting your partner get killed by a demon, then going to *work* for them is the action of a traitor," he snarled.

I gripped Reaver's pommel at my hip, anger radiating through me. "I didn't *let* him get killed. And what the fuck was I supposed to do?" The truth of the matter was I'd frozen when the attack happened. I'd been terrified, and only two weeks ago when I was taking down the vampire who was terrorizing Buxton did I find out that that same vampire had been the one responsible for my partner's death—all in an attempt to manipulate my actions into joining PIG. Yeah, I'd been pissed at the time, but after a couple of weeks of working with Sawyer and being put in more life-and-death situations than I'd probably ever experience in half a dozen lifetimes, I decided that supes were more loyal than humans could ever be.

"All right, folks, let's just simmer down," the EMT said.

I peered up at him and noted his name. "Jones, no offense, but stay the fuck out of this." I looked back at the hate-filled sack of shit in front of me. "Smith and I are just having a lover's spat.

Isn't that right?"

"Fuck you, McKenzie." Turning on his heel, he stalked back to his squad car and slammed the door.

When I turned back to Jones, he and his partner were sharing a look. After I caught his eye again, I tried to explain what had happened. "Smith is an insecure asshole threatened not only by my gender, but by my ability to work with the supes *without* developing any fucking prejudices."

"Look, I don't want to know the details of the beef, but this situation…" he swept his arm out to encompass the whole entry in Wonderland thing, "… is stressful enough without you two bickering."

"I think we were nitpicking but whatever."

I could tell he was holding back an eye roll. "Whatever it is you were doing, it's not helping. We'll be waiting inside the rig for when they come out with the body." Jones and his partner walked back to the ambulance, leaving me alone.

Sitting my ass down on the asphalt, I heaved a heavy sigh. I had no idea how long this was supposed to take, although if I had my necklace, I might have been able to help. How in the hell was I supposed to get it back?

The air shivered, then the sensation of spiders marching across my skin under my clothes made me leap to my feet. I narrowed my eyes at the stack of containers that marked the entrance to Wonderland, not seeing anything out of the ordinary.

It's fine, I tried to tell myself. As long as there wasn't a change in atmospheric pressure, I was fine.

Brushing at the invisible legs, I waited…

Waited…

Pop!

Oh, hell no.

Palming Reaver, I prepared myself for whatever the fuck Wonderland was about to spit out at me. I didn't think about the reasons *why* I wasn't dead right now since I was clearly in the realm of the fae. Spreading my feet a little more, I balanced my weight, focusing on my breathing—slowing it and my heart rate.

There was the scrape of shoes on the hard ground then…

"Oh, shit." Keeping my grip on Reaver, I dove to the ground to avoid being hit by a fireball. Kseniya's scream echoed the loud thump of the flames into the side of a container, and I quickly glanced over my shoulder to see that Smith, Jones, and his partner were still in their cars. They couldn't see this, so for now—at least—they were safe.

When I clambered to my feet, Kseniya was there, her brown eyes flashing with rage. She hurled another fireball at me, and when that one missed me by a hair's breadth, she shot a deluge of water from her cupped palms. It hit me in the chest, sending me flying backward. I hit the container with a grunt, all the air leaving my lungs in a mass evac order. Coughing, I blinked through my dripping hair to find Kseniya waving her hand around like she was casting a spell.

"I hate witches," I muttered to myself, scrambling to find my footing again. I'd just taken a step when the ground beneath me began to rattle. "Oh my God, what now?" I yelled.

Kseniya smiled at me and sprinted off, leaving me to look up at a cyclops that had just lumbered out from behind a container. It looked as if his body was decomposing. His skin was sagging on all the joints, his jowls dripping from his skull like melted candle wax. The putrid smell of carrion and old blood made me gag, forcing me to cover my nose with one arm.

"Why can't some things just be fictional?" I moaned. Maybe even a little petulantly.

The ground buckled under the weight, his footsteps leaving cracked asphalt in their wake. At least ten stories high, the cyclops lumbered toward me, the look of determination in his one rotting eye unnerving.

Unhappily, I uncovered my nose so I could ready myself as well as I could, bringing Reaver up in front of me. It heated in my two-handed grip, a comfort I needed now that I was fighting this thing alone. I eyed the cyclops's long arms and legs and wondered what kind of reach he had.

When the monster was about twenty feet away, he swiped for me with a grunt. Ducking and rolling, I quickly got back to my feet, then I slashed at his wrist. The sword cleaved through skin, muscle, and bone, the blade singing with the taste of blood. The melody was accompanied by the baritone bellow of the cyclops as he wrenched his bloody handless arm back. Blood spurted from the bloody stump, falling like thick oil and covering the ground in swimming-pool sized puddles.

He reached for me again with his left hand, grunting in triumph when he caught me by the foot. Hauling me up into the air, the cyclops brought me up so I was level with his eye. His fetid roadkill-esque breath suffocated me when he opened his mouth and lined me up like I was a tasty morsel.

Nope. I was *not* going out like this.

Curling into a vertical sit up, I thanked Mike once more for punishing us with crunches and brought Reaver down on the cyclops's finger that was holding me. I didn't get enough momentum on the swing, though, and instead of severing the appendage, I only pissed him off with a deep cut.

The cyclops roared in pain and let me go.

Shit. Shit. *Shit!* I had not thought this through. I was ten stories high. Hurtling through the air, wind rushed past my ears and tore at my clothes. I was free-falling with fear as my only companion.

Think, McKenzie.

As I fell past his coarse fabric shirt, I managed to grab a handful of the hem, dangling there for a moment before I could pull myself up. Pain streaked through my shoulder, the joint reminding me that it wasn't ready for lifting my body weight for another four to six months.

Tucking Reaver back into my belt, I hauled myself up the cyclops's shirt. He tried to swipe me off, black blood splashing me in the face from the ragged stump. I wiped what I could off my face, then dragged myself up onto his shoulder, the cyclops shaking his body like a wet dog the whole time in an effort to dislodge me.

My hands shot out to keep my balance, but instead of a handful of shirt, I got a handful of rotting skin that was sloughing away from the muscle and bone of his shoulder. Disgusted, I instantly released it, shaking my hand to fling off the gore, then tried again. This time, my fist enclosed around rough cotton and just in time too. The cyclops opened his mouth and let out another petulant roar, spittle flying from his lips.

I scrambled up the open neck of his shirt, barely avoiding his blind gropes as he tried to knock me off. I looked up—looked around—trying to figure out how I could bring the bastard down.

"Think, McKenzie, *think*."

There!

There had to be at least seven feet between me and where I needed to be. Scaling the bastard like a mountain, I pulled myself up onto his ear, balancing inside the giant silver ring through the lobe.

All of a sudden, the cyclops stopped moving and stood completely still. Maybe he was like a T-Rex, and he could only see movement? Cautiously, I stood, holding onto the loop and looked up. Brown, ropey hair was hanging above my head, but given the cyclops's skin had literally fallen off his body, I wasn't in a rush to use it to pull myself up with it.

How am I going to get to his eye? I wondered.

Reaver pulsed in my palm, and I looked down at the sword, a plan forming in my mind's eye.

"Please, God, let this work." Before I could kick my own ass for potentially making a stupid mistake, I threw the sword with all my strength toward the top of the cyclops's head.

A moment later, the cyclops shrieked in pain, bringing his bloody hand up to cover his eye. When the bastard stumbled back a step, I held on tight to the earring as he crashed to the ground. Foul-smelling black blood oozed out from between his fingers, pooling around his head at an alarming rate. When he finally stopped twitching, I stepped free of the earring and straight into the mess.

I lifted my foot—black, sticky strands sticking to the sole. "Jesus," I muttered, walking back a few steps. Looking up, I saw Reaver's pommel sticking out of the cyclops's eye. Then I wondered whose plan it had actually been to throw it up there—mine or Reaver's?

One problem at a time, I reminded myself.

Peering over at the EMTs and Smith, I saw them still in their vehicles, completely unconcerned. They'd either watched the whole thing with popcorn, or I was still in the protection of Wonderland's magic.

Walking toward them, I sucked in a breath when I got my spider-crawling sensation, the world coming back into existence and my senses with a *pop* that hurt my ears. Glancing over my shoulder, I saw the cyclops's body shimmer into existence too. The boundaries of Wonderland must've been snapping back into place, probably in protest from being manipulated in the first place.

The EMTs sitting up straight in their seats was my first clue they could now see me. Jones and his partner were out of the rig and running toward me a moment later, their eyes wide as they stared at the giant corpse.

"Jesus, what happened?" Jones practically yelled, easing me down onto the ground to check me over. He looked beyond me to where the cyclops had fallen, his poor human brain trying to piece together the tear in his reality. "And what the *hell* is that?"

"Just Cat, thanks. And I got bored of waiting. so I went to pick a fight with a zombie cyclops."

Jones shared a look with his partner, then startled when he returned his gaze to me. He jabbed his finger at the ground beside me. "What is that?"

Points to him for not sounding as freaked out as he looked.

I glanced down and smiled. "Oh, that's Reaver," I replied, picking up the sword. Swiping my thumb over the etching of my face, it disappeared from view.

"How?" Jones shook his head vigorously. "No. I don't want to know."

"All right, why don't we just check you over?" his partner said, moving Jones out of the way gently. "Jimmy, why don't you go and sit down?"

Jimmy did just that, shaking his head and muttering to himself on the way to the ambulance.

"Right, now that's he's out of the way," she said. "Let's take a look at you."

"You seem awfully cool with having the corpse of a cyclops within arm's reach," I told her. My eyes darted to her nametag. "Berman."

She looked up at me, then back at the graze on my arm. "I

always thought there had to be more out there than just us," she replied with a shrug. After a moment more of prodding, she said, "Just superficial wounds."

"Wow. Go me! I hardly got hurt that time."

"Does this happen a lot?"

"Only in the last couple of weeks," I replied. "Who knew being a cop was this insane?"

"I think if you weren't a member of PIG, it would be *less* insane."

Somehow, I doubted that. I think I was always bound to run head-first into crazy shit like this. She worked on cleaning the few grazes I had, then gave me a cloth to wipe the black blood from my face.

I looked over when there was a *pop*. Sawyer came out of Wonderland with Baba Yaga cradled in his arms. I hopped up immediately. If my partner was going to question me about the zombie, I wanted to be on my feet for it. I was short enough already and explaining myself from the ground always made me feel like I was a toddler.

"Do I want to know, pussy cat?" he asked wryly.

"Probably not." I shrugged. "But, hey, I won."

His lips quirked up into a slight smile. My stomach flipped at the sight of it, and I quickly refocused my attention on the old witch in his arms. She looked just the same as I remembered—like everyone's favorite grandmother—until she opened her mouth to reveal her shark teeth that ate her grandchildren. Her filmy nightgown was in tatters, hanging off her body in sheer ribbons. Her chest was carved with symbols that were now burned into my memory.

"Same as before?" I asked.

Sawyer nodded and turned his attention to the rattling of a gurney being hauled down to us. Jones's face was unreadable.

Berman took the head of the gurney as he arrived, steadying it, then unzipping the body bag. Sawyer put Baba Yaga's body onto it and zipped it up. He strapped her in and turned his eyes to both EMTs. "Don't touch the body without gloves on. She's very powerful. Wait at the clinic until the ME takes custody of the body. You should have the address of our facility." They nodded, then took Baba Yaga's body back to the ambulance.

"We have a facility?" I asked.

"We do now," Sawyer muttered, then turned his gray eyes to me. "I take it you're responsible for that dead cyclops."

"Maybe? In my defense, it was already dead… you know, given it was a zombie and everything."

He pressed his lips into a hard line. "It could've killed you."

I snorted, folding my arms. "Please. Have a little faith in my awesome abilities, Sawyer."

"Did it just wander out of Wonderland?"

"Nope. Our girl Kseniya sent him after me. I think she's still a little bitter over that beating I gave her."

"Oh, the beating that you came home from black and blue?" he asked, his brows arching.

I jabbed my finger into his chest. "I don't appreciate that tone," I snarled, then added softly, "but that's the one. Anyway, somehow, she manipulated the opening of Wonderland, and it crept forward to include me. Then she was there, throwing fireballs and torrents of water at me. The cyclops was her coup de grâce."

He ran a hand through his hair, fisting it briefly before releasing it. His eyes held the kind of torment that belied his casual air. I braced for some yelling. Maybe a couple of well-timed and burn-worthy curses, so I was unprepared when he pulled me to him, clutching me tightly.

Into my hair, he whispered, "Can you please stop putting yourself into these situations?"

Unashamedly, I inhaled the scent of whisky and chocolate from his body. I loved being this close to him, and the fact that we'd had sex only made it worse.

His arms tightened around me. "Promise me, pussy cat."

"You know I can't do that." Pulling away, I took a quick step back. "I'm a supernatural shit magnet." He did not look amused, so I gave him my best smile and added, "Hey, at least we know my necklace wasn't the thing responsible for letting me walk into Wonderland and not... you know... *die*."

My statement didn't seem to have the effect I'd wanted. "Come on. You need to eat to recover from your little jaunt into Wonderland, then we've got to get to the ME's office. Our new supernatural examiner will be waiting."

"We have one of those now, too?"

He nodded. "Got hired yesterday."

At least we were being heard.

The next thing we needed was a team of CSI who were supes.
And some undercover patrol cars.
Baby steps.

16

"Here, put this on."

A PIG jacket smacked me in the face, and I looked over at Sawyer. "Hey!"

He gestured to my own jacket that was splattered in black blood. "You need to change. Otherwise, you'll scare the nice humans when we go inside." *Inside* was the burger place we'd stopped at.

The last time I'd come out of Wonderland, it felt like someone had pulled the plug on all my energy, and Sawyer had had to practically carry me into the restaurant and force-feed me liver and pancakes. Yeah, it was as disgusting as it sounded.

This time around, though, I felt okay. More than okay, actually. Shucking my bloody jacket, I threw it at Sawyer, then slid my arms into the fresh one. Lifting the collar to my nose, I inhaled, catching his dark chocolate and whisky scent in the fibers. After Sawyer shoved my jacket into one of the saddlebags on his motorcycle, we walked toward the front door.

He ushered me inside, and we took a seat near the window, pulling the greasy laminated menus from the holders at the end closest to the window.

"So, who's our new ME?"

"His name's Doctor Julian Lee. Skin-walker. For over thirty years, he worked as an ME in Buxton before retiring a few years ago. Wolfe managed to convince him to come back and work for PIG."

"Go, Wolfe. But wait. What's a skin-walker?"

"In Navajo culture, they're a kind of witch doctor, who can disguise themselves as an animal. They're believed to be evil, to be able to control someone completely by just making eye contact, but like most things supernatural, it's all relative."

"I'm Flo," a bored-sounding waitress said, breaking into our conversation. "What'll it be?"

Flo had to be in her early sixties, her aged face hard and unyielding like she'd worked at this burger place since she was in her teens and she didn't take shit from anyone anymore—the punk-ass kid playing soda jerk behind the counter or the dicky deep fryer out back along with its short-order jockey.

"A cheeseburger with extra mustard and a soda," I said, sliding my menu back into place.

"Just a coffee," Sawyer replied.

I shifted my legs up onto the seat beside Sawyer. "So what

happened in Wonderland? Where was Baba Yaga's body found?"

"In what, I suppose, was her home." He pulled out his phone and showed me some photos. "Markings are the same, but like with Rose, there was no raven or its feathers."

I scrolled through the photos. "Maybe there are no ravens in Wonderland?"

"There are, but their feathers secrete a poison that kills in seconds. She must've known that. Stop on that photo."

I did, enlarging the image with my thumb and index finger.

"See how deep that one is? Down to the bone."

"What do you think it means?"

"I don't know."

"Coffee. Soda," the waitress announced loudly, placing the coffee in front of me and my drink in front of Sawyer. "Burger's coming."

When Flo shuffled off, we swapped drinks, and I took a long drag of my soda. "All right, so deeper cuts and no ravens. Do you think she's amassed so much power now that she doesn't need to use all the elements of the spell?"

Sawyer stirred his coffee silently, placing the spoon down on the table. "It would explain why she's changed her MO. Maybe she doesn't need the sacrifice anymore."

"And with each kill she's gaining a power."

"Cheeseburger," Flo said, placing the red plastic basket that was acting as a plate in front of me. "Anything else?"

She wandered off before I could ask about the double mustard. With a shrug, I picked up the burger and took a bite, then chewed.

Sawyer took a sip of his coffee, staring at me over the rim. "What I want to know is what's her motive for killing all these witches and stealing their power?"

Swallowing, I said, "Well, if I were her and my whole family had been destroyed, I'd be coming after the person who did it, but I'd make sure…"

Sawyer looked at me sharply. "What?"

"I'd make sure I was stronger than before," I finished, thinking it all through. "I'd guarantee my victory."

"Okay, let's see if this theory has legs. Kseniya's stealing the powers to go after the Morozovs in order to seek revenge? Is that what you're saying?"

"Yes, but nobody has heard from the Morozovs since the slaughter," I pointed out, taking another bite of my burger. "Kseniya wouldn't be doing all this now unless she knew where her quarry was. That's why she killed Sharyn… to steal the ability to find someone. I bet she selectively stole those other powers, too. Maybe they're more effective against whatever powers the Morozov she's hunting has."

"Do you have to speak with your mouth full?"

I grinned. "Yes, it helps me think."

He let out a sigh.

"We need to find and warn the Morozovs… wherever they are."

He threw me a speculative look. "We don't even know they're *here*. They could be anywhere in the world."

"Why wouldn't they be here? The entrance to freaking *Wonderland* is in Buxton. Why wouldn't a member of a powerful witching family be here, too?" I took another bite of my burger, licking mustard from my fingers. "How hard do you think it'll be to find them?"

"I think we're in needle-in-a-haystack territory."

"Be serious."

"I am. They could be using aliases or be anywhere in the world right now, despite

your supposition that they're here in Buxton."

"I'm telling you, at least one of them is here. Why else would Kseniya be spending so much time in Buxton? We just have to get to them before she does."

He drained the rest of his coffee. "Are you done?" He nodded at my half-eaten burger. "Lee is waiting for us."

Shoving the last bite of the burger into my mouth, I washed it down with a sip of my soda and stood.

Sawyer dropped some cash onto the table. "As soon as we're done with Baba Yaga and Lee, we can start tracking the other Morozov witches down."

TWENTY MINUTES LATER, SAWYER SLOWED THE DUCATI AND PULLED into the driveway of what looked like a very expensive private clinic, complete with an ambulance tucked neatly under an awning beside the building.

"This is the ME's office?" I asked Sawyer through the comms

in the helmet.

"Yeah. I don't know how Wolfe pulled it off, but PIG finally has an ME of our own."

Sliding into a parking spot opposite the entrance, Sawyer killed the engine, waiting for me to slide off the back before putting down the kickstand. After stowing the helmets, we walked through the steel and glass doors and into a modern office lobby.

A man walked out of a door beside the receptionist's desk and asked, "Detective Taylor?"

Sawyer held out his hand to the guy. "Yes. Doctor Lee?"

"Please, call me Julian," he replied, pushing his square glasses up his nose.

"This is my partner, Officer Cat McKenzie."

Lee turned his attention to me, his brown eyes kind. I automatically dropped my gaze. "Please don't worry about that, ma'am. I've never been good with mind control, and I have no interest in it either." He held out his hand to me. "Doctor Julian Lee."

Doctor Lee looked to be in his mid-thirties, even though his eyes hidden behind his glasses looked much older. It made me wonder what kind of lifespan skin-walkers had. However old he really was, it seemed puberty hadn't left him yet—his cheeks and jaw were covered in acne.

"Nice to meet you," I said. "I'm not a supe."

His brow quirked up. "Well, I won't hold that against you then." He gestured to the door he'd come through. "Are you ready to see the body?"

"No," I replied.

"Yes," said Sawyer at the same time.

Lee looked between us, a nervous smile appearing on his face. "Right. This way, please."

The skin-walker led us down a long hallway that ended with a set of double-doors. I let the other two go through first, needing a moment to collect myself.

"You all right?"

I nodded. "Yeah. Yep. Just need a minute."

"Take as long as you need," he replied, folding his arms and leaning back against the wall.

After letting out a breath, I nodded and followed him in, fighting the instinct to turn right back around and leave again. The smell was what got me—formaldehyde. It hung in the air pervasively, making my nose crinkle. The steel drawers along one wall, the wash-down white tile floor—complete with hose reels on the walls—and medical chandeliers hanging over two steel slabs in the center of the room only added to the creepiness.

Lee pushed the glasses up his nose. "I waited until you got here before I began the autop—"

I jumped when there was a loud *bang* from the wall of steel drawers. I looked at Sawyer, whispering, "What the hell was that?"

He frowned. "It sounded like it came from—"

Bang! Bang! Bang!

I yelped, pressing myself against the opposite wall from the steel drawers, the tiles hard against my shoulder blades. My heart was in my throat, my pulse thumping out a tachycardic rhythm. "Sawyer?" I asked, my voice warbling. Fuck. Keep it together, Cat. I couldn't act like a scared little woman in front of the new work associate. "What's going on?"

He pulled out his Glock and stepped forward. I shuffled to the side, my foot bumping into something and knocking it to the floor. It landed with a *clang*, the echo bouncing around the white-tiled room.

Sawyer's gaze flickered to me. "Are you okay?"

"Fine." I looked down. "It's Reaver."

If the sword was here, I probably wasn't going to like what was about to happen.

Scooping it up, I held it at the ready, ignoring the way Lee's eyes widened when he saw it.

"Where did… You didn't… How…" His mouth gaped.

"You get used to it," I told him, my eyes still on the wall of stainless steel. I was extra creeped out because the banging had been shoved into horror-movie territory with the addition of nails scratching and clawing at the door.

I swear to God, my heart stopped beating in my chest when Sawyer approached the drawers.

"Lee, which drawer is the body in?"

The skin-walker hustled forward and placed his hand on the handle of the second drawer on the left, about halfway up.

"On the count of three, open it then get out of the way," Sawyer told him, cocking his .22 and sliding his finger onto the trigger. With his free hand, he held up three fingers, then counted them down. When he made a fist, Lee opened up the drawer—immediately throwing himself to the side and out of range.

Sawyer fired three times, each hit making the corpse of Baba Yaga screech like a banshee. The slugs did nothing to slow the witch as she shoved herself out of the drawer and leaped at Sawyer. His grip on the gun loosened, falling out of his hand and sliding across the tile.

"Why isn't she dead? You said she was dead!" I yelled at my partner who was wresting on the ground with a corpse.

Sure, it was clear that she wasn't, but it was always good to talk these things out.

"She was." He grunted, prying back her arm and twisting at the same time, forcing the frail-looking-not-a-woman-but-really-a-corpse onto the floor. The two aprons of her skin flapped open with an audible *squelch* as she landed hard on her back.

Sawyer straddled her waist, holding her down by her shoulders. The witch's bloody abdomen was covered in the symbols Kseniya had carved into her body, but that wasn't what bothered me. It was the fact that Baba Yaga's throat had been cut open, leaving a gruesome carved smile in her gray, waxy skin.

"Cat," Sawyer ground out, dodging the witch's clawed hands, trying to peel off his face. "I need you to cut off her head."

I shook my head. "If I go to my therapist and tell her I decapitated *another* person, she's going to call the cops. And I *am* the cops. I'd have to arrest myself. Not cool."

He glared at me, his dark hair flopping into his face. Damn, he was looking sexy right now. "She's already dead. She's a zombie."

"A zombie?" I thought back to the cyclops I'd fought. "She doesn't look like a zombie. Her skin isn't all melty and foul."

"She's newly dead. The body hasn't decomposed yet. Can you stop arguing with me and just do as I ask?"

Hitching my hands onto my hips, I retorted, "Would it kill you to ask nicely? Argh, never mind."

As if it knew it was going to be used, Reaver heated in my palm, glowing a faint electric blue. Hoisting the sword above my head, I said a quick prayer then brought the blade down onto Baba Yaga's neck. The scent of burning flesh immediately permeated through the room, and I had to resist the urge to let go of the pommel and run screaming from the room.

"Again," Sawyer yelled at me, wrestling to keep the witch's body... err, corpse... still.

Yanking hard, I freed Reaver, sending a stream of black blood arcing through the air. It spattered onto Sawyer's shirt, Baba Yaga's face, and my cheek. Wiping off what I could onto my jacket, I swung the blade again, bringing it down onto her neck—onto the same spot as my first strike.

This time I hit bone. There was a fizz and a *pop,* and her head separated from her body. Baba Yaga's clawed fingers slackened. Her arms dropped from Sawyer's shoulders, falling limply to the floor beside her.

Sawyer clambered off the body, blood coating his shirt and pants.

"D-d-detective Taylor, are you okay?" Lee asked in a stammer from behind us.

"Fine, Lee," Sawyer replied, wiping the blood from his face.

Lee's dark eyes darted to the dead-dead witch on the white tile. "I'm glad you two were here for this. I don't think I could've handled *that* on my own."

I saluted him with my bloody sword. "Anytime."

"Cat, help me get her body back onto the slab," Sawyer asked.

"Ooo, hard pass. Cadavers and I don't mix. I should know. I've created enough of them in the last few weeks."

He rolled his eyes at me and looked to Lee, who quickly took the shoulders while Sawyer grabbed Baba Yaga's feet. Even though it squigged me out, I picked up her head by the hair and placed it gently at the top of the slab where it would've gone before her unfortunate post-mortem decapitation. Hey, it was the least I could do considering I'd been the one swinging the sword.

"Sorry about the mess, doc." I gestured to the glossy black blood on the floor.

Lee only smiled, pushing his glasses up his nose. "No problem. That's why the floors are tiled and we have hoses."

Eww. "Okay. Great."

"I think I'll get the autopsy done tomorrow," Lee said, pushing his glasses up again. "That is, unless you need a cause of death right now?"

COD — decapitation, I thought wryly.

Sawyer said, "Tomorrow will be fine. I just wanted to meet you and let Cat get a look at the body. Photographs are one thing…

it's quite different to see the injuries in person."

"I couldn't agree more," the doctor said.

"I just wish I hadn't had to see them in action, too," I grouched. Turning to Sawyer, I raised my brows at him. "Can we go now?"

"Yeah." Turning to Lee, he said, "Nobody will claim her body. After you're finished with her, cremate the body, and I'll collect the urn."

As we left, I said, "Do you have a creepy collection of urns at your apartment I need to know about?"

He gave me a sideways look that could've meant so much. "Just get on the bike," he growled, sitting astride and kicking the engine into life.

I did as he asked, trying to ignore the black blood that seemed to have soaked into every inch of his clothing.

"Where are we going?" I asked into the comms of the helmet.

"Home. I need to get showered and changed. You should probably do the same."

Yeah, I guess he had a point.

17

"Cat? Cat, you need to wake up."

I rolled over and swatted Sawyer away. "No sex right now," I mumbled. "Too tired."

"Jesus," he muttered then hissed, "*McKenzie.*"

I bolted upright, almost headbutting Sawyer in the process. Blinking, I stared at the clock. Three in the morning. "Why am I awake at three in the morning?"

"I just had a phone call from Amy."

"Well, good for you. Enjoy the booty call." Yep, I sounded grouchy about that, but as I tried to roll back over and shut my eyes, Sawyer ripped the blanket from my body and hauled me out of bed. His heated eyes dropped to my silky unicorn print camisole before returning to my face.

"Amy Elliot," he said. "The witch we spoke to on Monday. She said we needed to get over to her house right now."

"A threesome *is* on my fantasy list, but not with someone in their fifties, and not a woman. Being the meat in a man sandwich is more my style."

He shook me, my teeth clacking together. "This isn't about sex or feeding," he ground out. "She said she knows where Kseniya is."

Suddenly awake, I scrambled from the bed, then quickly got changed, throwing on a pair of jeans and a long-sleeved tee. Plucking my PIG jacket off the hanger, I slid my arms into it as I shoved my feet into my boots. Just as I was about to leave, I grabbed the warded cuffs—the ones that would stop and subdue almost any supe in their tracks. Sawyer always said I ran into situations without thinking. Well, I was thinking today.

Scooping my hair into a ponytail, I secured it at the top of my head and found Sawyer waiting for me by the door. We left without speaking, the reality of the situation finally settling over me. Sawyer pushed his motorcycle hard, speeding through the empty streets of Buxton on the way to Amy's house. I didn't want to think about how Sawyer knew where it was. Jealousy was sludge in my veins when I thought about him with any other women, but as I'd told myself a thousand times before, Sawyer wasn't mine to own.

I'd done him a solid when he really needed it.

We had our one-time-only sex, and now it was done.

When he pulled the bike to a stop against the curb, I yanked off my helmet and looked at the house we'd parked in front of.

"There are no lights on," I said.

"It's not that house," he replied. "I parked about a block away just in case Kseniya shows up."

Together, we walked the block to Amy's house. It was freezing this early, the air bitingly cold, and the ground was slick with ice. I slid a little on one patch, only being saved from taking a nose-dive when Sawyer curled his hand around my arm and kept me upright.

"Thanks," I breathed, smoke from my breath settling in the air.

He nodded, and we kept going. It was too quiet, the sound of it deafening in the pre-dawn light. When we reached a little rancher set back from the street, I looked up and down the street. There was nobody else around, and no lights were on in the other houses. Amy's house was dark too.

"Are you sure she said to come over n—"

An enormous fireball erupted from the building, blowing through a front window and serenading the night with the tinkle of broken glass. The shockwave rippled through all my senses, making my bones quake, my ears ring, and my nose bleed. My skin came alive with magic.

Wiping the blood away with the back of my hand, my hearing came back online. I turned when I heard the car alarms. Every car in the street—probably the county—had been set off by that blast, and I watched as light after light was turned on in the houses.

"Shit." Sawyer was moving toward the house before I could

stop him. Drawing his Glock, he eased slowly through the partially opened door, and I followed, covering his back—and mine—by shutting us inside the witch's house.

There was no need for innocent people to get sucked into this little melee.

Cold air swirled into the room, the ball of flames that had gone through the window redecorating the living room floor with dangerous shards of glass and splintered wood.

Very nouveau chic.

I looked up, scanning the rest of the room and faltering to a stop.

Now, I'll be the first to admit I was expecting to find fluffy kittens cross-stitched onto cushions and lace-frilled curtains in shades of pink and mauve in Amy Elliot's house. I mean, the woman wore scrubs with cat footprints on them.

I was not prepared for the matte black walls, the blood-red carpet underfoot, ritualistic daggers, black candles, black feathers, and crystals scattered on every flat surface or the pentagrams hanging from the walls.

And was that *blood* on the coffee table?

Behind my ribs, my heart started to gallop. Amy was supposed to be a natural witch—a *white* witch—so everything I was seeing didn't fit with my preconceived notions.

I jumped when Reaver suddenly popped into existence and fell onto my foot—

pommel first—before thumping to the ground. Stooping, I picked it up, my eyes slamming shut as a rush of bloodlust hit me, twisting through me like a tsunami tide.

Startling when Sawyer touched me on the shoulder, I stared into his eyes, dragged his whisky and chocolate scent into my lungs. "Are you okay?"

"Fine," I gasped. "I think Reaver is a little pissed off with Kseniya. I just got a *really* strong emotion of bloodlust."

His eyes darted to the blade that was glowing faintly in my hand. "How… strange."

I would've picked another word, but sure, let's roll with *strange*. Jerking my head toward the dark open doorway, I said, "Let's go."

Moving like shadows, we inched further into the living room, both of us hardly breathing. The faint glow Reaver was giving off would be our only giveaway, but so far, I could hear and see nothing. As we shuffled over the carpet, raven feathers stirred and broken glass tinkled past our shifting feet.

A light came on in the room beyond the living room doorway, making us both stop. Sawyer turned to look at me, half of his face bathed in golden light and the other casting his face in shadow.

Then there was a hiss. "This is for the death of my family, *suka*."

"Kseniya," I mouthed to Sawyer.

He nodded, bringing up his Glock and creeping forward another inch to peer around the corner. After a moment, he waved me forward.

Easing up beside him, I let out a breath when I saw Amy laid out on her dining room table, her arms and legs tied down with rope and the front of her pajamas ripped open. Kseniya was standing over the other witch, a dagger in her hand and blood dripping from three gouges on her cheek. Amy had obviously put up a fight.

Amy struggled against the ropes, the veins in her neck and forehead bulging. "I don't know what you're talking about."

Kseniya cackled, the sound like fingers down a chalkboard. "Do you think I'm an idiot? Do you think I wouldn't remember your face?" She ran the tip of her dagger down Amy's cheekbone and chin like a lover would trace a finger in the heat of passion. Her skin split and blood dribbled, oozing down her neck. "I remember. I will *always* remember the face of the woman who helped hunt down my family, who sentenced them all to death. I *know* who you really are, Amy Morozov."

Morozov? I gripped Sawyer's wrist and squeezed, silently asking him whether he knew Amy was a Morozov. Subtly, he shook his head, and I released my hold.

Gaze flickering back to the tableau, I watched Kseniya bring the blade up in front of her face. She licked the blood from the steel, her eyes shuttering in ecstasy. "You're just the first, Amy, but I'm going to hunt them all down and make them suffer like I've suffered."

"You'll never find them."

"That's where you're wrong," Kseniya crooned. "I've already got their locations. All of them. New York, Sydney, Kabul, Sofia, two in Vienna. I know where they are."

"You're lying."

"Am I?" Kseniya asked, her mouth pulling into a smug smile. She reached into her pocket and pulled something out, throwing it onto the table beside Amy's face—away from our line of sight. "Recognize who that once belonged to?" she asked.

Amy moaned plaintively, her head falling to one side.

"Your dear brother told me everything… where I could find you, where you lived and worked. He told me of your name change and how every single one of his female relations went into hiding after you *slaughtered* mine." Kseniya looked off into the middle distance. "I can still hear his screams." She smiled down at Amy. "And now I will hear your screams."

Tears mixed with the blood that was still streaming from the wound to Amy's face, covering her pale cheeks in thin crimson slashes. Her eyes were glazed with pain, with fear. But then her unfocused gaze cleared when she saw me, then Sawyer. She opened her mouth, croaking, "Help… me."

I glanced at Kseniya to see if she'd heard Amy's plea for help. She hadn't—she'd turned around, searching for something on the sideboard.

We could get her now, while Kseniya's back was turned. Reaver flared hot in my palm. Apparently, *it* liked that idea. I took a step forward, but Sawyer grabbed my arm and shook his head. He pointed at himself instead, then motioned for me to go through the adjacent door, which joined from what I guessed was the kitchen.

Even though it killed me, I backtracked into the living room and went to find the other entrance. Walking down a short hallway, I stopped at the spill of light on the carpet and peered past the jamb. The kitchen was empty, but I could see Kseniya's shadow moving across the tiles.

"Buxton PD," I heard Sawyer say. "Drop the dagger. Keep your hands where I can see them."

I stepped into the kitchen, my shoe squeaking on the tile as I slipped on some blood.

Kseniya hissed.

Sawyer shouted, "Kseniya Chernov. It's over. Drop the dagger!"

There was a beat of silence. Kseniya laughed—a cruel, mad sound.

Then…

… Amy gasped sharply.

Screamed.

And screamed.

And screamed.

Sawyer pulled the trigger on his Glock just as I ran the rest of the way. Bursting from the kitchen, I watched as Kseniya wrenched the dagger from Amy's chest before plunging it back in again, seemingly uninjured from the point-blank shot Sawyer had just fired into her chest. Sawyer's jaw was tight as he pulled the trigger again, his fingers around the grip blanching.

Kseniya brought up her hand and made a flicking motion, causing his whole body to go loose before it slammed into the wall—it was as if a giant invisible hand had simply swept him out of the way. His head made a sickening *thunk* on impact before he crumpled to the floor.

With a smile, Kseniya turned to look at me. "I'm not interested in anything but getting my revenge. You should take your partner and leave."

"Sorry, but I'm not in the habit of giving in to the whims of bad guys," I said with a shrug, my gaze darting down to the table to see what Kseniya had shown Amy. It was a finger, shorn off just below the base knuckles. On it was a large gold men's ring.

"Suit yourself." Kseniya held out her hand—palm toward me—then closed her fist. Intense pressure wrapped around my arms, legs, and torso, a giant hand squeezing. With a strangled gasp, I tried to move, but I was locked in place. My heart lurched in my chest at the thought of being trapped here, then Kseniya pulled my opal out of the top of her shirt. I couldn't stop the heartsick whimper escaping me.

Stay calm, McKenzie. Can't let the bad guy know how much you want something.

Amy started making gurgling sounds, her mouth moving soundlessly. The red-headed witch leaned down to listen, and the smile that bloomed on her face was terrifying.

She ran two fingers through the blood spewing from Amy's chest wound and brought them to her mouth with a satisfied purr. "I can taste your fear. It hums through my bones, through my blood."

"Leave her alone," I yelled, struggling against the arresting spell she'd cast on me.

Kseniya turned her cruel dark eyes to me. "You can't stop this. This has been thirty years in the making."

"Blah, blah, blah, I know. Jeez, you bad guys always like the sound of your own voice." I needed to buy myself some time here. The longer she played with me, the easier she'd be to apprehend because surely someone had called the cops by now.

Her gaze shifted down to Reaver, which I still had in my hand—my palm locked around the hilt. "You stole that from me," she snarled.

"Hate to break it to you, babe, but you were the one who stole it from me. In fact, I think you have a little problem since you also pilfered my necklace that same night."

Kseniya touched the chain around her neck. "You have no idea what that opal can do, do you?" she asked with a sneer. "It's wasted on an ignorant human."

She said 'human' like a germaphobe would say 'dogshit.'

Trying not to look like I was struggling, I ground out, "I have a feeling you're going to tell me whether I like it or not."

"It's a conduit. It amplifies my powers. That's just a bonus, though. The real reason I wanted it was for…" She paused theatrically.

"Protection…" I breathed. It had protected me that first time we fought, deflecting her attack…

… but not the second time.

I frowned. "Why didn't it deflect your fireballs that night on the street?"

"I wasn't trying to kill you that night. I was merely attempting to wear you down. I suspected the stone worked that way, but only after that night did I know for sure."

I thought back to every volley she'd sent my way. They'd crashed into the wall behind me or beside my head, but not once had she hit me. In fact, she sent most of the fireballs wide.

She brushed the opal with her fingertips. "Magic like this can't be taken from a corpse. It can either be stolen or given freely. And it worked just as I'd hoped with the Douser and the Reaper. No matter what they threw at me, it repelled it all."

The Douser?

"Rose Sanchez?" I asked.

The Reaper was an easy one to figure out.

Kseniya nodded.

"So, all these witches you butchered and stole magic from were to gain power in order to kill one little Echo?"

Kseniya laughed—even threw her head back as if I was so damn hilarious. "Is that what she told you?" She gestured to Amy. The other witch's chest had stopped rising and falling a few minutes ago. "She's a Seeker."

"What's the difference?"

"One is light, and one is dark. Amy *Elliot* is as dark as you can get."

I looked down at the woman we'd spoken to only days ago. Then, she'd been wearing obnoxiously bright and cheerful pale pink scrubs with navy blue paw prints. She looked like a kindly grandmother, but I was beginning to realize supernatural beings used great camouflage.

Baba Yaga was a prime example of things-you-shouldn't-fuck-around-with.

"Don't let her appearance fool you. At the age of twenty-five, *she* was the ruthless leader of her family's coven."

"I sense a bit of jealousy," I sing-songed.

Kseniya's eyes flashed with sudden anger, her mouth narrowing into a thin slash. "She was the one who found each and every one of my family members and had them slaughtered. She was the one who sentenced them to unimaginable cruelty and pain. *She* is supposed to be the first in a long line of deaths. I'm going to cut off the head of the snake before I slaughter the rest of them!"

Even though it was hard to breathe, I had to keep her talking. I *had to* hold out a little longer. Sawyer was still motionless on the floor. "And what about you, huh? How did you escape that slaughter thirty years ago?"

"My father took me away and hid me."

"And who was he?"

"A fae named Dain. He protected me while they hunted down my mother's blooded kin."

"And that's how you got into Wonderland," I surmised. "With the strength of his blood in your veins?"

"Yes," she hissed.

Behind us, in the living room, someone kicked in the front door. I would've pumped my fist in the air if I could have. Finally, *finally,* something was going my way. Shifting my eyes to the doorway, I waited…

Then cursed when I saw who it was.

"What are you doing here?" I demanded breathlessly.

Kailon Perry stood in the doorway, his green eyes as cold as the wind blowing in from the broken window and as sharp as the jagged glass still in the casement. He stalked closer, his usual glamor disappearing to reveal iridescent scales, slitted bright green eyes, and a forked tongue which darted from between his still-human looking lips every few seconds.

"I've come for my pound of flesssh," he replied, his syllables drawn out and long in a viper's voice.

Kseniya smiled at him like the cat who got the canary. "The Conjurer. The full-blooded fae. I was surprised to stumble across her. She was much more powerful because of her pure blood and far more powerful than a human witch. I just had to have her." She touched her mouth. "You know, I can still taste her blood on my lips."

"I will draw thisss out," Kailon hissed. "I will make you sssuffer."

Kseniya squared her shoulders and faced him. "Come and get me, then."

The invisible band around my chest disappeared, and I dropped like a stone, my head bowed as I tried to catch my breath. As I was panting on my hands and knees, I realized Reaver was gone. *Again.*

Looking across the room, I saw Sawyer stir, his eyes moving behind the lids but not fluttering open yet. The side of his face was covered in blood thanks to the head wound he'd received when he got a little intimate with the wall.

Kseniya conjured up a fireball, the flames licking at her skin yet not burning her. She launched it at Kailon with a self-satisfied grin on her face. Wind was suddenly whipping through the dining room, pushing me back down onto the floor. I managed to peer up, though—just in time to see the fireball that Kseniya had launched at Kailon extinguish into nothing.

The witch tried water this time, sending a deluge at the fae from her outstretched palms. Once more, Kailon used his ability to shove the torrent away, although I could see the strain on his face in the way he clenched his jaw, by the sweat beginning to bead on his brow.

On and on they went, Kseniya attacking and Kailon on the defensive. I used their focus on each other and crawled under the dining table, watching them from relative safety. I couldn't stop either of them even if I wanted to, so like a mother with a toddler having a tantrum in a supermarket aisle, I let them have at it.

I soon realized Kailon was only playing with the witch, making her do all the work.

Did that mean he knew there was a bottom to her power?

Would she eventually just run out of steam?

But Kseniya didn't slow.

She didn't stop.

She just kept going.

On the other side of the living room doorway, I saw a couple of Buxton's finest creeping forward with their guns drawn but not aimed. They obviously didn't know who was who and whether they'd survive breaking apart something like this. One of the officers saw me crouched under the table, and I shook my head, motioning for them to stay back.

He nodded, relaying the information to his partner. When they disappeared from sight, I sent up a thank you that it wasn't Smith who had responded. That fucker would've got some popcorn and relished in watching me fail.

I had to stop this.

But how?

I glanced down when I felt something cold press against my leg. Reaver was lying against my thigh like a nervous dog pressing against its owner. Reaching for its pommel, I brought it in front of me. Kailon was staring at me when I glanced back up. With a grim set to his jaw, he began to advance on Kseniya.

The witch shuffled back a step, then another, moving closer to the table. When she was within range, I slashed at her ankles, hoping to cause her just enough pain to break her concentration. Kseniya grunted and fell, glaring at me through the curtain of her red hair.

"*Suka!*"

She lunged but fell short when she was dragged backward. Her hands scrambled to find purchase on the carpet, her nails sharpening to claws. Spinning over onto her back, she snarled like a tiger at Kailon, who slammed his foot onto her chest. Wind began to whip around them. Like a mini-tornado, the wind picked up speed, bits of debris flying into the swirling funnel that was concentrated just on the dining room.

The gale intensified, filling my ears with white noise that roared like a beast.

"Kailon!" I screamed, scrambling out from under the table. I wish I hadn't because a piece of broken window frame slammed into my stomach, doubling me over. I clutched at my middle, sucking in gulps of air. From my prone position, I peered through the howling wind to find Kseniya gasping for air and clutching at her throat. Pitiful mewling sounds escaped her as Kailon ruthlessly teased all the oxygen from her body, slowly suffocating her.

"Kailon!"

Shuffling forward, I tried to grab his arm, but he shrugged me off, shoving me back to the floor. Glass bit into the palm of my hand, but I had bigger things to worry about.

I held Reaver to his throat. He turned to me then with his serpentine eyes slitted and hissed.

"We had an agreement!" I screamed, forcing myself closer to him. The wind lashed at me, snapping against my face like the end of a whip. "We had an agreement!" I repeated. "And the fae always honor their agreements."

I saw the moment he faltered. I *felt* the moment he faltered. The wind that had been screaming around us before was now barely buffering me. Kailon hissed at me again before releasing his hold on the witch. The tornado disappeared, leaving papers, wood, and bits of glass littering the floor. Kseniya curled into a ball at his feet, clutching at her throat and trying to drag air back into her body.

Keeping one eye on Perry and the other on the witch, I pulled out the cuffs from my back pocket. Laying Reaver down beside me, I rolled the witch over onto her front and pulled her arms back, her hands resting at the base of her spine.

I secured one cuff on her wrist and was about to secure the other when Kailon shoved me out of the way. I tumbled backward, hitting the wall this time. Fuck, I was going to be black and blue after tonight. I wrenched my head around in time to see Kailon snap the other cuff around Kseniya's wrist, flip her over, then wrap his hands around her throat.

I opened my mouth to remind him of our deal again, but this time, he turned to me and said in an ophidian hiss, "There isss no more deal, Catherine Ellen McKenzie."

"This isn't what the fae do. You're breaking your word. The queen will kill you for this. You're in the human world."

"But you're the only witnessssss. All you have to do is ssstay quiet about it. Report that you were the one to kill her when ssshe resssisted arressst."

I looked down at the cuffs that stopped all her magic abilities. With them on, she was as helpless as a human. "That story won't fly if she's cuffed like that."

Kailon growled at me. "You're making thisss harder than it hasss to be."

I wrestled with the idea that maybe he was right. Kseniya had violently killed seven witches and who knew how many more. She had tried to murder Sawyer and me in a flood. She'd sent a zombie cyclops after me, and a gremlin to squash my car. The bitch had stolen my necklace—maybe I could just let this happen and nobody would know.

But *I* would know.

And if I let a monster kill a woman, and I was complicit, what would that make me?

Wrapping my hand around Reaver's hilt, I stood and pressed the sword to Kailon's throat. "No."

"*No?*"

"No. I won't let you kill her. I won't let you take her into Wonderland to kill her. She's still a human being, and she will be tried for the murders of Sara Fitzpatrick, Sharyn Wyatt, Samantha Giles, Rose Sanchez, and Amy Elliot… Chernov … fuck, whatever her name really is."

"What about Moira Whitethorn and Baba Yaga? Don't they dessssserve justice?"

"Wonderland is out of our jurisdiction. You said it yourself. If Kseniya had been caught in there, you would have all the rights to deal with her as you wanted. But she's here, in the human realm, and as such, she will be tried in the human realm. These are the rules, Kailon. Now, unwrap your hands from her throat, or I'll arrest you for interfering with an investigation and conspiracy to commit murder."

We stared at each other for a long while, each wondering who would break first. I had no intention of backing down from this. I was not the monster Smith thought I was. I was human, and no matter how deep I sank into the supernatural world, I always would be human.

Slowly, the fae unwrapped his fingers from the witch's throat, but his eyes remained slitted.

"You've made a dangerousss enemy, Cat McKenzie." His voice was like razor blades.

"Yeah, well, so have you, Kailon Perry. Now get out of here before I let Reaver have a taste." The wind picked up, and I pushed the sword in a little harder, dimpling his skin. With a roll of my eyes, I added, "Without the theatrics, please. It's been a long-ass week."

The air grew still immediately. The fae stepped back, threw one final dirty look over his shoulder, and disappeared.

Kseniya's brown eyes rolled in my direction.

"Just because I saved you from him, doesn't mean you're really saved. You've been a bad witch, and it's time to be punished."

I read her the Miranda rights, then got her up on her feet. Sawyer groaned as he came around, pulling himself up into a sitting position. Touching the side of his head, he grimaced, then looked from me to Kseniya then back.

"What did I miss?"

I waved my hand through the air like a debutant. "Oh, you know, the usual… fae versus witch. I hid under a table, took on Kailon, made him my enemy, then arrested Kseniya here."

"You made an enemy out of Kailon?" he replied. "How is that… no, don't answer that."

I grinned. "Now that you're not sleeping on the job, would you mind calling in the cavalry?"

Sawyer pulled the phone from his pocket and began dialing, cradling his head as he spoke.

I turned to Kseniya. "I believe you have something of mine." Reaching into her shirt, I pulled out my necklace. The stone heated in my palm, a sense of calm rippling over me. Undoing the clasp at the back, I returned it to my neck, letting it settle between my collarbones.

"You'll regret—" the witch started, but I stopped her with a hand in the face.

"Your plans for mass genocide were thwarted by a chick with teal hair and a sass mouth. Get over it, babe."

18

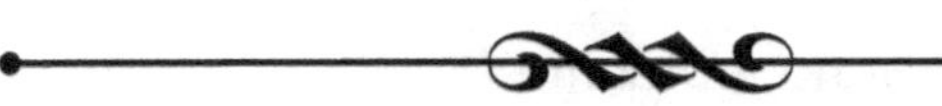

"And that's how my knee got fixed," I told Joanna Wong on Friday afternoon at our therapy appointment. "Who knew gnomes did more than decorate your garden?"

"Fascinating," she replied, not bothering to make notes about that. "And how are you feeling about everything now? I know it's only been a couple of weeks since you've had such a huge change in your life, but how are you adjusting?"

I looked down at the throw pillow in my lap. It was a new one. The word 'breathe' had been cross-stitched into it. "New pillow," I commented.

Yup, I was totally stalling on this.

"Yes. Do you like it?"

I nodded, tracing my finger on the big 'B.' I did as the pillow suggested and took in a deep breath then let it out. "I'm worried."

"About what?"

I looked up into her dark, almond-shaped eyes. "Losing myself."

Setting aside her notepad, she recrossed her legs and gave me her full attention. "In what way?"

I didn't want to admit that all of Smith's jibes had finally landed on their intended targets, but I was beginning to think he was right. I *did* prefer working with the supes, even if my initial fears should've made me run in the opposite direction.

"I'm afraid I'm losing my humanity."

"What makes you say that?"

"Well, I guess I'm concerned that I prefer to hang around with supes now. I'm never going to go back into the department."

"Why not?"

"Firstly, they don't want me. They're still attached to this stupid idea that I let my first partner die… *on purpose*. Which is ridiculous because there's no way I would let someone die for shit and giggles."

"We've discussed this before, though, Cat. Your partner's death, including your inability to save him, stems back to your mother's, then your father's deaths. They were mysterious, and you had nobody to blame for them. When the supernaturals came out, they were as good a target as any because they were scary and one hundred percent capable of doing it. When your partner died, you froze because you felt just as powerless then as you did when your parents died."

I knew all this.

I'd come to terms with these facts.

"The other thing is, I don't want to go back. I love working with Sawyer. I love the team. Although it's small and terribly under-resourced, I feel like we make a difference."

"And you do. I see the news articles all the time, where you and your partner are named in them. You're doing good work. You want to know what I think?"

"God, yes, that's what I pay you for."

"I think *you* haven't really come to terms with these changes yet. Now, just hear me out. You started a new career, and the whole idea in your head of catching bad guys was taken away when your partner died and you were reassigned. I know you see PIG as some sort of punishment, but I think it's a way for you to grow as a person as well as professionally."

I grunted. It wasn't that I didn't believe her, it was just that I wasn't *ready* to believe her. I was unhewn clay, not ready for the potter's wheel just yet.

"Cat, I want you to acknowledge this, okay?" Joanna pressed. "This is important. The other sessions you've come to, you've been cagey with me, which I understand. I've asked you to spill some of your darkest thoughts to me, but you know next to nothing about me. But I'd like to think that I've gained some of your trust and you're ready to start opening up to me more?"

I glanced back at the pillow then set it aside. "Okay, you want some dark thoughts? Here's my biggest one right now. Whose side am I on?"

"In what regard?"

"I mean, am I human or am I…" I paused. I wasn't a supe, but there were so many things about my life that were unexplained. The fact that my parents were part of a secret organization that hunted down and killed supernaturals before supernaturals were even known to be real. The fact I had a necklace that was a conduit for power. The fact I could step foot into Wonderland and not keel over a second later.

"Or?" Joanna prodded in that gentle, softly spoken voice of hers.

"Or am I one of the monsters?" I whispered.

"What makes you think you're one of the monsters?"

"One of the guys at work, Smith, he keeps calling me a traitor to humanity because I work with supes."

"And what do you think about him calling you that?"

Shifting in my seat, I curled my legs up under me. "What do I think? I think he's a jackass, but I also think… that maybe… he's right?"

She nodded and picked up her pen to make a few notes. "In your mind, is being a monster a good or bad thing?"

"Bad."

"Why?"

"Because that's the way they're always portrayed. The bad guys always lose. The good guys always win."

"Is it always about winning or losing, though?"

I shook my head. "Yes. No. Fuck, I don't know." Sucking in a breath, I let it out, then looked Joanna in the eyes. "Yesterday morning, I had to decide between an easy choice and a hard choice."

"What were these choices you had to make?"

"I could either let someone kill another in retribution, or I could choose to bring this person who killed so many to justice in the human courts."

"Who wanted to kill whom?"

I smiled, thinking that Sawyer would approve of Joanna's grammatical prowess. "A fae seeking revenge for the death of his niece and a witch who, oddly enough, was also seeking revenge for the deaths of her entire family."

"What we have here is the perfect example of two wrongs don't make a right, don't you think?"

"I guess."

She smiled a little. "And what was your choice?"

"I chose to let the justice system do what it was designed to do… punish the guilty, free the innocent."

"In your heart of hearts, do you feel like that was the right thing to do?"

"Absolutely. But now I have a very angry fae gunning for me."

Her eyes widened. "You think he would do you harm?"

"Oh, absolutely. He's like a dog with a bone. I took it from him, and he's going to want his chew toy back."

Joanna tapped her pen against her knee. "This is quite serious."

If only she knew who the fae was. I was sure I could get Joanna to swear then. "Yeah, and it brings me back to whether I did the right thing."

"If you hadn't done what you had, a woman would've been killed without a fair trial, without judgment."

"Yeah."

But Kseniya was as guilty as they came. She'd confessed to everything. She was going to jail for a very long time, but Kailon Perry wasn't, and he knew exactly where I lived.

I SHUT THE APARTMENT DOOR BEHIND ME. WHAT I'D SPOKEN ABOUT to Joanna during the session was cutting laps in my head. I'd have to be on my guard all the time from now on. Dropping my keys onto the kitchen counter, I started down the hall to my room to get changed.

"Cat?" Sawyer called from the living room. "Can you come in here for a second?"

Heaving a sigh, I backtracked through the kitchen and found him sitting on the couch dressed in sweats and that stupid body-hugging Under Armour shirt again. Seriously, why did he have to look so good? His hair was carelessly tousled, the stubble on his jaw delicious. But it was his eyes that seemed to hold me in place—those gray eyes that swallowed me whole. Now that I knew what was under all those clothes and the ferocity in his eyes, I was damn well powerless to resist.

"Cat," he growled.

"Yeah?"

His eyes darkened, flashes of lightning arcing through his irises. "Don't look at me like that." His tone was harsh, his words like a slap in the face.

"Okay." I waited for him to say something more, but he just

sat there with his jaw tight and his brows drawn low as if he was irritated by something. "Look, if you have nothing else to say to me, I'm going to take a shower. Therapy left me feeling icky."

I turned, took one step, then was tugged to a stop. The heat from Sawyer's body was at my back, causing me to shiver.

"I'm sorry," he murmured into my ear. "I didn't mean to bark at you like that, but I'm riding a pretty thin edge right now."

Turning to face him, his eyes swirled with shadows. I couldn't help but note how my breathing had suddenly become erratic. "When was the last time you fed?"

He inhaled sharply, taking a step closer. "Wednesday morning."

Wednesday? That was with me. "You haven't fed since then? Why the hell not?" My gaze drifted down his neck. His pulse was throbbing against his skin like it was a little animal wanting to get out.

He shook his head, a feral, hungry look in his eyes. "I don't want to feed off someone else. I only want you, Cat."

I swallowed. "I thought it was a one-and-done thing?" My question was raspy—needy—but I didn't care.

He flexed his hips into me, his erection thick and long on my stomach. He was hard. For me. I looked down and swallowed, licking my lips even though I shouldn't be encouraging this.

"How? I mean, I know *how*, but how is this possible? You're aren't supposed to be able to get it up for me again."

He smiled faintly. "Such a way with words." Pushing some hair behind my ear, he lingered there for a moment, his fingertips soft against my neck. "I don't know. It's never happened before. The only thing I can think of is because it's you."

I snorted, then clapped my hands over my mouth. "I'm not a special cupcake."

"You are to me, Cat." He stepped away, taking with him the warmth of his nearness, his whisky and chocolate scent. "But I understand if you don't want to go there again with me. We have a good thing going. Sex would only ruin it."

I wanted to reach for him, but I stayed where I was. I could have more of Sawyer, and he could have more of me, but was that the best thing for our professional relationship?

Deep down in my heart, I knew it wasn't.

He looked at me intently. "I guess I just wanted you to know."

Sawyer was waiting for me to answer, but my answer wasn't going to be the one he wanted to hear. Sawyer had lived for over one-hundred-and-fifty years. One-hundred-and-fifty years of sleeping with a different woman every night. One-hundred-and-fifty years of longing to be with just *one* woman.

And it turned out, I was that woman. I just had no idea how it had happened.

"Sawyer," I began, his name a broken whisper on my lips.

He shook his head. "Cat, you don't have to say anything. I understand."

"No, you don't," I replied. "I want you. Call me crazy, but I want you so badly, but what will it mean? Will we be fuck-buddies, or is this a relationship? If it's a relationship, what happens when it goes south, or I get jealous because you're unconsciously feeding off women, or, or—"

Sawyer touched his finger to my mouth, silencing me for the first time ever in our working relationship. "It's okay." Leaning forward, he kissed the side of my mouth then grabbed his jacket from the hook by the door. "Don't wait up for me, okay?"

And with a sad smile that hit me right in the heart, he left the apartment in search of a random woman to have emotionless sex with.

BAD WITCH

A CAT MCKENZIE NOVEL

www.ingramcontent.com/pod-product-compliance
Lightning Source LLC
Chambersburg PA
CBHW030751190726
48285CB00003B/810